"Maybe We Shouldn't Worry About Words."

He felt her quiver, almost heard her questioning her own resolve. But she didn't bawl him out. Didn't move away.

Rather, still looking ahead, she lifted her chin and said, "I think we should go back."

"Anything you want." His lips brushed a line up to her lobe. *Anything at all.*

Gently he turned her head until they were gazing into each other's eyes, noses touching. She quivered, but not from the cold.

"Would it surprise you to know," he said, "that I've always wanted to make love on a beach under a full moon with a batch of turtles ready to hatch?"

A smile touched her eyes. "What a coincidence."

He twirled his nose around hers, stole a featherlight kiss from one side of her mouth.

"Cole, when I said something might happen, I didn't mean this."

His hand on her arm, he brought her closer.

"I did."

Dear Reader,

When my editor asked if I'd like to submit for my very own series, I jumped at the chance! I love linked books and knew precisely what the stories should offer.

Foremost passion and unforgettable characters. Then a fast-paced plot along with a good dollop of drama—the kind of intensity that revolves around dark secrets, big family and glamorous settings.

Roll that all together and you have The Hunter Pact, a series based upon a billion dollar media conglomerate, Hunter Enterprises, and the warring siblings who run it. This first installment—*Losing Control*—is eldest brother Cole's story.

The word leader was created for Cole Hunter, along with tags like *loner, workaholic, defender* and even *misunderstood*. When a sassy nothing-new-to-offer producer is employed without Cole's knowledge, he chooses responsibility over instant attraction. There's enough on his plate, including tracking down his father's would-be assassin.

But Taryn Quinn knows what she wants and won't quit till she gets it. Much depends on her success in launching her project with Hunter's. She's prepared to do anything to achieve her goal…and I do mean *anything*.

I hope you enjoy *Losing Control!*

Robyn

Stay up to date here: www.RobynGrady.com

Follow Robyn on Twitter @robyngrady

ROBYN GRADY

LOSING CONTROL

HARLEQUIN®
entertain, enrich, inspire™

This book is dedicated to the friends I made during my
own days working in the media. Never a dull moment!

With thanks to my editor, Shana Smith, for her support
and work on this book and The Hunter Pact series.

ISBN-13: 978-0-373-73202-9

LOSING CONTROL

Copyright © 2012 by Robyn Grady

Recycling programs
for this product may
not exist in your area.

www.Harlequin.com

Printed in U.S.A.

ROBYN GRADY

was first published with Harlequin Books in 2007. Her books have since featured regularly on bestseller lists and at award ceremonies, including a National Readers' Choice Award, a Booksellers' Best Award, CataRomance Reviewers' Choice Award and Australia's prestigious Romantic Book of the Year Award.

Robyn lives on Queensland's beautiful Sunshine Coast with her real-life hero husband and three daughters. When she can be dragged away from tapping out her next story, Robyn visits the theater, the beach and the mall (a lot!). To keep fit, she jogs (and shops) and dances with her youngest to Hannah Montana.

Robyn believes writing romance is the best job on the planet and she loves to hear from her readers. So drop by www.robyngrady.com and pass on your thoughts!

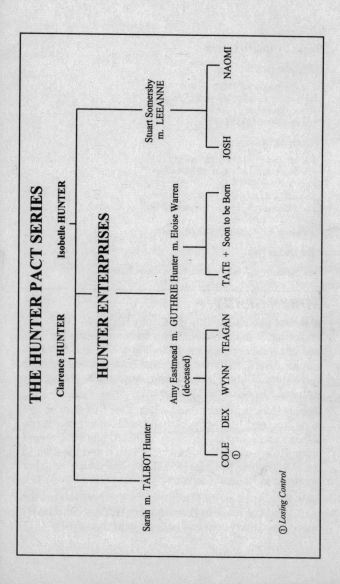

THE HUNTER PACT SERIES

Clarence HUNTER Isobelle HUNTER

HUNTER ENTERPRISES

Sarah m. TALBOT Hunter

Amy Eastmead m. GUTHRIE Hunter m. Eloise Warren
(deceased)

COLE ① DEX WYNN TEAGAN

TATE + Soon to be Born

Stuart Somersby m. LEEANNE

JOSH NAOMI

① *Losing Control*

One

Eyes shot up and all conversation ceased as Cole Hunter burst in and let loose a growl. Cole wouldn't apologize. He abhorred being kept in the dark, particularly when the deception concerned the man he respected most in the world.

Once, Cole's father had been a corporate powerhouse, a leader to be admired and, frequently, feared. More recently, however, Guthrie Hunter had softened. The responsibility of running Hunter Enterprises had fallen largely upon Cole's shoulders. The eldest of four, he was the person family leaned upon in a crisis, whether the drama unfolded here in Sydney or at one of the other Hunter offices located in Los Angeles and New York City.

Cole didn't want to think about that ongoing drama in Seattle.

His father's personal receptionist flew to her feet. With a look, Cole set her back in her seat then strode toward colossal doors that displayed the flourishing Hunter Enterprises emblem. How the hell could he keep things well oiled and on track if he wasn't informed? *Dammit,* he couldn't fix what he didn't know.

Cole broke through the doors. Turning to close them again,

his gaze brushed over the three openmouthed guests waiting in the reception area, one being a woman with wide summer-blue eyes and flaxen hair that fell like tumbles of silk on either side of her curious face. His raging pulse skipped several beats before thumping back to life. Work in television production meant beautiful ladies day in and day out, but true star quality was one in a million and this woman had it in spades. She must be auditioning for a show, Cole surmised. A special project if Guthrie Hunter planned to conduct the interview himself.

Something else he knew zip about.

His jaw tight, Cole slammed the doors shut. Swinging around, he faced the polished hardwood desk, which had prefaced that wall of glittering awards for as long as Cole could remember. Unperturbed, a silver-haired man sat in a high-backed leather chair, receiver pressed to an ear. Cole's sources said three hours had passed since a second attempt had been made on his father's life. Guthrie had probably wondered what had kept his firstborn so long.

Stopping dead center of the enormous office suite, Cole set his fists on his hips. Despite broiling frustration, he kept his tone low and clear.

"Whoever's responsible won't see light outside of a prison cell before both poles have melted." When his throat uncharacteristically thickened, Cole's hands fell to his sides. "For God's sake, Dad, shots were fired. This guy's not about to stop."

Guthrie muttered a few parting words into the mouthpiece then set the receiver in its cradle. Surveying his son, he tipped his clean-shaven chin a notch higher.

"I have this under control."

"Like you had it under control a month ago when your car was run off the road?"

"The authorities concluded that was an accident."

Cole looked heavenward. *God, give me strength.* "The license plates belonged to a stolen vehicle."

"Doesn't mean the accident was an attempt on my life."

"I'll tell you what it does mean. Bodyguards until this is sorted. And I don't want to hear any argument."

When Cole went too far and shook his finger, Guthrie's smooth expression fell. Sixty-two-year-old palms pressed upon the desk and Guthrie pushed to his feet with the agility and posture of a man thirty years younger. Cole's jacketed shoulders rolled back. There wasn't a man alive who could intimidate him, although, even now, with an ax to grind, his father came close.

"You'll be happy to know I have organized a bodyguard," Guthrie said. "He's a private detective, as well."

Absorbing his father's words, Cole willed away the red haze rimming his vision. His temper dropped a degree and then two. Flexing his fingers at his sides, he blew out that pent-up breath.

"What were you thinking, keeping this from me?"

"Son, I've only just got in." Rounding the desk, the older man crossed over and set a bracing hand high on Cole's jacketed arm. "You have enough to worry about. Like I said… everything's under control."

Cole winced. Guthrie was kidding himself.

Four years ago, when his father was recovering from bypass surgery and Cole had turned thirty, the family empire had been sectioned up and each son designated an equal portion to manage. Here in Sydney, Cole manned the Australian television cable and free-air interests. When he wasn't chasing skirt, Dex, the middle son, looked after the motion picture end of business in L.A. The overindulged, overachiever and youngest of the Hunter boys from Guthrie's first marriage, Wynn took care of the print media slice of the company from New York. Cole's remaining full-blood sibling Teagan was off doing her own thing in Washington State.

Initially Cole had bristled at the idea of Daddy's Girl shun-

ning her responsibilities and refusing to step up to help run
the business. Hunter Enterprises had provided well for them
all, Teagan's childhood operations and college designer gowns
included…although, to be fair, with the top three jobs filled,
her role would need to be a subordinate one. But given the
time he spent watching and worrying over his brothers' business and personal decisions, Cole had to be grateful that the
Hunter wild child had opted out. God knows he had enough
to deal with.

Of course Cole still loved his brothers and sister. Nothing
could ever change that. They'd shared a wonderful mother,
a talented Georgian beauty who had beamed whenever she'd
told a new acquaintance that both he and Wynn had been born
in Atlanta. With only two years separating each, the Hunter
children had grown up tight. But, thanks to gossip magazines
and the Net, all the world knew about the rifts, which made
the running of such a vast enterprise under separate helms
even more of a challenge. Through Dex's overindulgence and
Wynn's overzealousness, Hunter's reputation had taken some
blows recently. For everyone's sake, Cole was determined to
assume genuine leadership over every quadrant of Hunter
Enterprises, or die trying.

Guthrie wanted his children to mend their fences, get along
and continue to build together. With their father married a second time to a calculating woman, playing happy families—
keeping it all together—was nigh on impossible.

Winding away from his father, Cole moved to an early-
spring view of commuter ferries crisscrossing Sydney Har-
bour's vast blanket of blue.

"I'd be happier speaking to Brandon Powell about organizing full-time protection," he said.

"I know you and Brandon have been friends for years, and
his security firm is one of the best. It's not that I didn't con-

sider it… But, frankly, I need someone who's clear on who's paying the bill."

Cole pivoted around. "If you're suggesting Brandon would ever act unprofessionally—"

"I'm saying you'd be at him to divulge every detail of my every move, including what transpires beneath the sanctity of my family's roof, and that is not an option. I know you don't approve of Eloise, but—" Guthrie's furrowed brow eased and, weary of that particular fight, he exhaled. "Son, my wife makes me happy."

"As happy as my mother used to make you?"

"As happy as one day I hope you will be with someone you truly care for."

Cole refused to acknowledge the sheen in his father's eyes or the uncomfortable restriction in his own chest. Instead, he headed back to those massive double doors. Lust and love were two different states. A man his father's age should know better. His eldest son certainly did.

As if to highlight the point, the first thing to catch Cole's eye as he strode back into his father's reception lounge was that blonde and her star quality coaxing him into her long-legged, lush-lipped orbit. What red-blooded male would pass on the chance to bring those amazing curves close, to sample the soft press of that body and sweet scent of her skin? But that urge was sexual, only lust.

One day, Cole hoped to find the right woman. Someone he'd be proud to call the mother of his children. Someone he would respect and receive respect from in return. His stepmother didn't know the meaning of that word. In fact, he wouldn't be surprised if Eloise was behind those bullets for hire. Despite his father's edict just now, he had no qualms about finding out if Brandon Powell thought the same.

When his father's voice broke into his thoughts, Cole blinked his attention away from Ms. Summer-Blue Eyes.

Standing to Cole's left, Guthrie was studying him, salt-and-pepper brows hitched at a quizzical—or was that approving?—angle.

"I see you've met our new producer, Taryn Quinn."

Cole did a double take. Producer? As in *behind* the cameras as opposed to in front of them?

Again he examined the woman whose glittering gaze was pinned directly on him. Feeling his blood swell, Cole cleared his throat. Producer, talent…either way, it made no difference. If his father hadn't discussed this before now, anything other than a cursory introduction would have to wait. He had a meeting to attend, important documents to sort.

Cole muttered, "Good meeting you, Ms. Quinn," then prepared to shove off. But she'd already eased to her stiletto-heeled feet, and as she extended a slender hand, the light in her eyes seemed to intensify tenfold. Dazzling. Inviting. Cole couldn't deny he felt the warmth of that smile to his bones.

"You must be Cole," she said as, reaching out, his fingers curled around and held hers. A current—subtle yet electric—sizzled up his arm and, despite his ill humor, Cole found a small smile of his own.

Well, guess he could spare a moment or two.

"So, you're a producer, Ms. Quinn?" he asked.

"For a show I approved last week," his father interjected as Ms. Quinn's hand fell away. "Haven't had a chance to speak with you about it yet."

Cole asked, "What kind of show?"

"A holiday getaway program," Taryn Quinn said.

Out of the corner of his eye, Cole caught Guthrie fiddling with his platinum watchband the way he did whenever he felt uncomfortable. And rightly so. The last holiday series Hunter Broadcasting had piloted died a quick and deserved death. In these tough economic times, if viewers were to swallow yet another "best destinations" show, the promise would need to deliver fresh sparks week after week.

And what about the exorbitant budgets? Sponsors could pull down costs but, since the global financial crisis, any collaboration was a squeeze. Despite her obvious allure, if the decision had been his, Cole would've given Ms. Quinn's idea the thumbs-down before she'd cleared the gate.

Another mess he'd need to clean up.

From behind her desk, Guthrie's receptionist interrupted.

"Mr. Hunter, you asked to know if Rod Walker from Hallowed Productions called."

Thoughtful, Guthrie stroked his chin before heading back toward his office. He paused beneath the lintel of that massive doorway.

"Taryn, I'll drop by and touch base soon. In the meantime…" His focus swung back to his son. "Cole, I've allocated Ms. Quinn the office next to Roman Lyons. Do me a favor."

Cole thrust both fists into his trouser pockets. He guessed the favor. No way would he raise his hand.

"I have a meeting—"

"First, see that Taryn's settled." Guthrie's light expression held while his voice lowered to a steely tone Cole knew well. "Your meeting will wait."

Taryn nodded her thanks to Guthrie Hunter then turned to his Hollywood-attractive son. Her jaw tightened even as her heart beat a thousand miles a minute. How women must melt at Cole Hunter's feet. How they must dream of his smile.

"Your father's a considerate man," she said as Guthrie's towering doors clicked shut, "but if you're busy, please don't let me keep you."

When she resumed her seat, crossed her legs and reached for a magazine, rather than run with the offer, Cole Hunter remained rooted to the spot, and for so long Taryn began to wonder whether he'd expected a curtsy before heading out.

Her gaze crept up from the fashion section.

In that rich graveled voice that made her stomach muscles flutter, he explained, "I can't put this meeting back."

"Oh, I understand."

She sent a quick smile he didn't return. Rather, the crease between the dark slashes of his brows deepened. "My father shouldn't be long. Rod Walker's a busy man, too."

Taryn nodded affably, recrossed her legs, and the magazine took her attention again. But as she flipped to the gossip pages, she was aware of the younger Mr. Hunter checking his wristwatch then shaking his jacket sleeve back down.

"My guest's flying back to Melbourne at midday," he went on. "We don't have much time."

Glancing back up, she cocked her head and blinked. "Then you'd best hurry."

Cole Hunter wasn't hard to work out. Foremost, he was get-out-of-my-way ambitious, which she understood. Nothing compared with the buzz of landing on top, achieving a true sense of financial and personal security. She'd grown up with an aunt. One of Vi's favorite sayings was, *At every turn, in every way, invest in yourself,* which meant achieving a good education, grabbing regular exercise, staying loyal to friends and, wherever possible, dodging "trouble." Which brought Taryn to Cole Hunter's *second* quality.

Clearly, he was an intensely sexual being and, for whatever reason, she had piqued his interest. The testosterone pumping through his veins, darkening those ocean-green eyes to a storm, was as tangible as the breadth of his chest or square set of his jaw. The man exuded a masculine energy that stroked Taryn's skin and stirred a delicious aching heat low in her belly.

Understanding these things about Cole Hunter was the reason for her reservation now. She didn't care who he was, what he thought of himself, how many women he'd bedded, with how much skill or how little effort. Certainly she wouldn't be rude, but *Guthrie* Hunter had hired her and no matter how knee-knockingly sexy, if the son was ambivalent, hell, she'd survive.

As she held her honest-you-can-leave look, Cole shifted his weight and those incredible eyes narrowed as if he were now seeing her in a somewhat different light.

"Actually," he finally said, "that office next to Roman's is on my way." When she opened her mouth to decline, he overrode her. "I insist."

He extended and continued to offer his hand until, knowing she was cornered, Taryn accepted. As expected, the same fiery trail that had flown up her arm the first time they'd touched sparked again—not that she let any hint of the rush dent her poise. She made certain her eyes didn't widen, that her breath didn't hitch. And yet the satisfied grin smoldering in Cole's eyes said that he knew what she felt because he felt it, too.

As they moved toward the building's main thoroughfare side by side, she imagined Aunt Vi holding up her hands in warning and shaking her head. Taryn agreed. Cole Hunter was one of those "trouble" spots. Hotheaded, superior, radiating sex appeal like a supernova gave off light and heat.

Thank God they wouldn't be working together.

Two

"Guthrie would've mentioned we'll be working together."

When his statement received no reply, Cole wasn't entirely surprised. Taryn Quinn was attractive and charming. She was also aloof. Mysterious. As they walked together down the eastern wing of the Hunter Broadcasting building, Cole admitted he was intrigued, as his father knew he would be.

Rod Walker's call was an excuse Guthrie had pounced upon to bring his son and new producer together, despite the fact that Cole was, one, hard-pressed for time and, two, obviously opposed to investing in Ms. Quinn's proposal. Money was too darn tight and Guthrie knew it. But when she'd seemed so indifferent toward him—sitting there demurely with those shapely legs crossed, engrossed in that glossy magazine—blast it, he'd been intrigued all the more. Against better judgment, he'd decided to escort Taryn to her office and see if he couldn't prick that haughty shell.

So far, no good.

Passing an interested group of employees, and still awaiting a response, Cole risked a glance. Taryn was staring at him as if he'd announced science had proven that the moon was indeed made of green cheese. Perhaps she was hard of hearing.

He spoke louder. "I said as long as you're with Hunter Broadcasting, you'll be working under me."

"I'm sorry." Shrugging back slender shoulders draped in an elegant black jacket, she looked dead ahead. "But you're wrong."

Cole's step faltered. Not deaf. Nor had she misunderstood. He threw a suspect glance around. Was there a hidden camera or was she purposely ruffling his feathers?

"You must be aware of my position here—CEO as well as Executive Producer—and that's for every show that comes out of Hunters. I give the nod on budgets, sponsor deals—" his gaze sharpened on her perfect profile "—as well as the overall vision of any given project."

The peaks of her dark blond brows arched as she met his gaze square on. "Guthrie and I have discussed all that. I'll be working directly beneath *him*."

Cole didn't hide his smirk. He disliked cruelty in any form but he might enjoy setting sassy Ms. Quinn back, flat on her pretty behind. Whatever Guthrie had said, he hadn't worked in that kind of hands-on capacity for years.

Or maybe he should look at this collusion from a different angle. What had Taryn Quinn said or done to get this close to his father? And exactly how close was that?

Suddenly a dozen other questions sprang to mind, like where did Taryn hail from? What was her personal background? Did she have a criminal record? Did she know anything about those murder attempts?

Up ahead, London-born Head of Comedy, Roman Lyons, was strolling out of his office, whistling that same Cockney tune that grated on Cole's nerves like nails down a chalkboard. When Roman first joined Hunters, the two had a disagreement over the direction of a series. Cole had terminated his contract. Guthrie, however, had persuaded Cole to give Lyons another chance. After two years, Cole would concede that Roman did a good job. He'd even stepped in to oversee things a few times when Cole had been called away. But they'd never be best buds.

Now as he and Taryn approached, Lyons issued a casual salute to Cole, but his focus was fixed on Taryn. From the awareness sparkling in Lyons's dark hooded gaze, anyone might think that he knew her.

"This must be the new girl. Taryn, is it?" Lyons offered a knowing wink as well as his hand. "Word gets around."

Cole's jaw jutted. Word hadn't gotten around to *him*.

"Thanks for the welcome," Taryn said as her hand dropped away. "And you are?"

"Name's Roman Lyons."

"Looks like we'll be neighbors, Mr. Lyons. I drew the office next to yours."

"I was about to grab a cuppa," Lyons went on. "Can I tempt you?"

Taryn's face lit. "I'd kill for coffee."

"Let me guess," Lyons said. "White, one sugar."

Cole growled. *Oh, give me a break.*

"I'll leave you two to get acquainted." He started off. "I have work to do."

"With Liam Finlay? I saw him headed toward your office a minute ago." Roman straightened the knot of his tie as if he were loosening a noose. "He didn't look happy, if you don't mind me saying."

Cole bit back a curse. Liam Finlay wasn't a man to keep waiting, particularly today. Finlay was CEO for Australia's most popular football league. Hunter Broadcasting had held the cable broadcast rights to the majority of that league's games until five years ago, when Guthrie and Finlay had suffered a major falling-out. This year those coveted rights were back up for grabs. Cole had had a hard time getting Finlay to even talk. At this juncture, he couldn't afford any perceived insults, like letting his guest sit around twiddling his thumbs.

In a near-sincere tone, Taryn said, "Thanks for taking the time, Mr. Hunter. I'm sure I'll be fine from here."

A pulse point in Cole's temple began to throb. He had to get to that meeting. But, dammit, he wasn't finished with Ms. Quinn just yet.

As Roman sauntered off, Taryn entered her new office, which was decked out with teak furniture and the latest tech equipment, including visual and audio state of the art. But she moved directly to the floor-to-ceiling windows. He imagined he heard her sigh as she drank in the billion-dollar harbor view, complete with iconic coat-hanger bridge and multistory-high Opera House shells.

Letting his gaze rake over the silken fall of her hair and the tantalizing curves concealed beneath that smart blue skirt, Cole leaned a shoulder against the doorjamb.

"You have qualifications other than in television production, Ms. Quinn?"

"I've worked in TV since attaining my Arts Business degree."

"Then you'd have experience—held positions—in other areas within the industry, correct?"

"I started out as a junior production assistant and worked up through the ranks."

"And my father was—" he scanned her skirt again "—suitably impressed by your credentials?"

When she angled around, her smile was lazy, assured. "As a matter of fact, Guthrie was more than impressed."

"I make a point of having all my employees' backgrounds screened, management particularly."

"Heavens, you must have skeletons jumping out of closets all over the place."

His mouth hooked up at one side. *Cute.*

He crossed his arms. "Any skeletons in your closet, Ms. Quinn?"

"We all have secrets, although they're rarely of interest to anyone else."

"I have a feeling I'd be interested in yours."

Those big blue eyes narrowed then she strolled up to him, the deliberate sway in her walk meant to challenge. When she was close enough for the scent of her perfume to tease his nostrils, she stopped and set her hands on her hips. Cole exhaled. Poor Ms. Quinn. Didn't she know he ate novices like her for breakfast?

"I've taken up enough of your time," she told him. "Don't keep your guest waiting. I'm sure your father will be along soon."

He grinned. Damn, he could play with her all day, if only he had the time—which he didn't. He pushed off the jamb.

"My father might have employed you, but I'm the one in charge of the books, and if your show doesn't perform, production stops. That is, if I allow it to get off the ground in the first place."

A shadow darkened her eyes. "My show will not only launch, it will be a new season smash. We're bringing in A-list guests."

"Been done."

"Choosing destinations that are considered rough as well as luxurious."

"Old."

"The host I have in mind is the most popular in the country. Voted Australia's most eligible with a string of hits under his belt."

Cole's gaze flicked to her naturally bee-stung lips. "That's the best you can offer?"

He imagined her quiver, as if a bolt of red-tipped annoyance had zapped straight up her spine. "I have a signed copy of the approved proposal as well as a contract setting my salary."

"A contract which will be paid out unless your pilot is fresher than tomorrow's headline news."

An emotion akin to hatred flashed in her eyes. "Perhaps I should put a call through to my lawyer."

"Perhaps you should."

Any space separating them seemed to shrink while the awareness simmering in that steamy void began to crackle and smoke. Taryn Quinn whipped up his baser instincts to a point where he could forget she was an employee. In fact, right now he was evaluating her through the crosshairs of a vastly different lens. She pretended to be cool, in control. Would she be so restrained in the bedroom? Instinct said she'd set the sheets on fire.

She was saying, "And if I were to come up with something you hadn't seen before?"

He gifted her with a slow smile. "Then, Ms. Quinn, I'd be happy to visit it."

He asked that she get the original and revised proposal to him as soon as she had something that would knock his socks off. But as Cole made his way down the corridor toward his office and Liam Finlay, he berated himself. Normally in these kinds of situations he wasn't distracted by sex appeal; that was playboy Dex's vice. But the challenging blue depths of Taryn Quinn's eyes, the impudent tilt of her slightly upturned nose, the fact he knew in his gut she was hiding something…

Thinking of those flaming sheets, Cole admitted, he was looking forward to prying open her closets.

"What do you think of the Commander?"

Familiarizing herself with her office LCD TV, Taryn glanced up. Roman Lyons had returned with two steaming cups in tow. Remote control in one hand, she accepted the

coffee he offered while she grinned at Roman's nickname
for Cole.

"Cole obviously likes to run a tight ship," she conceded.

"As much as he likes introducing newcomers to his infa-
mous plank."

"Sounds as if you speak from experience."

"Cole has his fans—" bringing the cup to his mouth,
Roman arched a brow "—as well as his foes."

"Which side do you fall on?"

"On the 'keeping my job' side. To survive in this industry,
you need to roll with the punches. But you've been around.
You'd know all that." He nodded at the static on the screen and
gestured at the control. "This office was vacant for a while.
I'll tweak the settings."

She handed over the control and watched as he concentrated to tune in channels, including internal feeds. Roman
Lyons was good-looking in a saucy Hugh Grant kind of way.
Certainly friendly, helpful and with a sense of humor, too. No
wonder he rubbed "Trouble" the wrong way.

"Tell me how you came to be at Hunters," Roman said, as
his thumb danced over the remote's keys.

"I had a long stint at the last network I worked for." She
mentioned the name and recited a few of their shows. "Last
year, one of the executive producers asked for ideas for new
series. He was interested in a couple of mine but ultimately
passed. In the meantime another network approached me."

"The industry does like to poach."

"I declined their offer of an interview. I was happy where
I was. But management heard about the communication and
when information about a new show was leaked, they ques-
tioned my loyalty." Remembering the scene when that EP had
dressed her down, she shuddered and blew out a breath. Her
direct boss was livid at his protégée's treatment, but he had a

family to feed. She'd insisted he not get involved. "That afternoon, my desk was packed up and I was out on the curb."

Roman collected a second control off the stand. "TV is not for the faint of heart."

"I could have filed a suit for unfair dismissal. But I decided to rise above it, take the payout and move on."

"What happened to the network that wanted to poach you?"

"That position was already filled. But I knew my ideas would fly somewhere else. After wallowing for a couple of weeks, I plucked up the nerve to call here and speak to Guthrie directly."

As she took a sip from her cup, Roman handed back the first control. "Good for you."

"Frankly, I almost fell off my chair when he asked me to come in for an interview. I was even more blown away when he gave my show the green light straightaway." Thoughtful, she ran a thumb over the remote's keys. "I was on such a high, so convinced I'd do a great job, but after meeting Cole, I have to wonder if that green light is fast turning red." She set the remote down on the corner of her desk. "Roman, can you set me straight on something? Because I'm a little confused. Which Hunter is in charge here? I know control of the branches of the company was split a few years ago between the three sons, but I assumed Guthrie still pulled all the strings."

Beneath a flop of dark sandy hair, Roman's high brow creased. Then he held up a cautionary hand and, although they'd been speaking quietly, he crossed to close the door.

"Word is that after his wife's death," Roman said, moving back, "Guthrie lost all heart. No one knows for sure, but if you put it to a vote, most will say he gave up all control."

"You mean Guthrie has *no* say? What's he doing then, hiring me?"

"Guthrie was down for a while but when he married again, he got his wind back. Staff here were chuffed. It was as if he'd got another chance at life and he didn't intend to waste a minute. The wedding was big, expensive—" he hiked a brow "—and fast."

Of course Taryn remembered the publicity surrounding that big day, a huge celebrity bash with a bride who had looked thirty years the groom's junior—which was nobody's business but their own.

"At my interview, Guthrie seemed genuinely excited and behind my show," she said.

"Then he must believe in it."

"While his son's hand is twitching on the guillotine rope. He told me unless I can come up with an extraordinary twist, I'm out."

Roman thought for a long moment before giving a mischievous smile. He purposefully set down his empty cup. "Right-o. We need sketch pads. Markers. A plan."

She blinked and then brightened. "As in *you* and *me* 'we'?"

"Two heads, and all that. What say we come up with a twist that hits Cole right where he bloody well lives? He'll either love it or…"

"Or he'll love it." He *had to*. Taryn moved to scoop her laptop out from its bag. "Let's get started."

Three

When Cole stabbed the loudspeaker key and realized who was on the phone, he flung down his pen and grabbed the hand piece. It was past six—closer to seven. He'd been hanging out for this call all day.

"Brandon, thanks for getting back to me."

"Just got back into the country." Brandon Powell's familiar deep drawl echoed down the line. "What's up?"

Cole gave his friend a summary of events—the attempt to run his father's car off the road three weeks ago, the near miss with shots fired this morning, how Guthrie, to his mind, didn't appreciate the seriousness of the situation.

"You want to fix your father up with protection," Brandon surmised.

"He's already hired someone."

"Then I'm not sure what you want me to do."

"For starters, put a trace on Eloise."

"Your father's *wife?*"

"Second wife." Cole's lip all but curled. "I have a hunch she might be behind it all."

"You're accusing Eloise of attempted murder—based on what?"

"Based on the fact she's a—"

Cole let loose a few choice adjectives and nouns that had been building for years, starting when he'd first got wind that a much younger woman—a so-called family friend—was making a play on a man who'd recently lost a loving wife. None of the boys had thought Guthrie would be interested in her batting lashes and syrupy condolences. When it had become apparent the two were an item, their father was already hooked.

Brandon's reply was wry. "I take it you haven't warmed to your stepmother yet."

"I still can't believe he married her. My mother's best friend's gold-digging daughter."

Shame on Eloise but more shame on his father.

"I hate to mention this," Brandon said, "but Guthrie's an adult. He makes his own decisions."

"And I make mine. How soon can you organize a tail?"

"If you're sure—"

"I'm sure."

"Give me a few hours to track down the right guy and brief him. But I need to warn you. If your father has his own man on the job, there's a chance he'll find out you've done this behind his back. And if Eloise ultimately isn't implicated…"

Cole knew what his friend had left unsaid. Guthrie took the well-being and loyalty of his entire family seriously. His father had a five-year-old son with Eloise and another on the way. If he discovered his eldest had gone behind his back like this, he'd view it as a betrayal. Guthrie wouldn't disown a son, but he might kick Cole out of Hunter Enterprises for good.

Considering the options, Cole rapped his fingers on the desk before he drove down a breath and confirmed, "I'll take that chance."

He didn't want a rift to develop between two more members of the Hunter clan but, dammit, his father's safety came first.

After settling some details, he and Brandon caught up

briefly. Brandon was still enjoying his bachelorhood and was looking forward to a Navy Cadets reunion; they'd served in a unit together for three years rising up through the ranks from "dolphins" to petty officers. Brandon said he hoped to see Cole there, but he'd be in touch before then.

They signed off and, feeling worn out, Cole set his bristled jaw in the cup of his hand at the same time his empty stomach growled. He hadn't eaten since breakfast. There was still more he could do here tonight, but his brain needed fuel. Time to knock off.

While Cole shut down his laptop, a knickknack perched on his desk caught his eye. The winding steel-tube-and-rope puzzle had been a gift from Dex and was based on the Gordian Knot legend. Thousands of years ago, Alexander the Great had been asked to unravel that intricate knot, which everyone knew couldn't be done. But Alexander had thought outside of the box and found a simple solution. He sliced through the rope with his sword and, *hey presto!* With this gift, Dex was telling Cole to lighten up…life's problems didn't need to be so intense and all-consuming.

Cole would rather ignore advice from a playboy producer who was overdue a Hollywood hit. There *were* no shortcuts to success. No easy paths to victory. Cole kept the toy on his desk not as a reminder to take the low road as Dex was wont to do, but as a prompt to stay on course, even when he might rather say *to hell with it all*.

After shrugging into his jacket, Cole locked up his office, spun around and near jumped out of his skin. In the muted light, he'd almost run into something. Or rather, someone.

Taryn Quinn stood not a foot away, her scent still fresh, her eyes still bright. With her blond mane gleaming and plump lips bare of gloss, she looked like a vision. A drop-dead sexy vision, at that.

She inspected his briefcase, peered around his frame to the closed door and her eyes widened in alarm.

"You're leaving?"

He frowned. "Didn't realize I had to sign out."

"I thought that someone in your position would be here till all hours."

When Taryn lifted the open laptop she held, the penny dropped. She'd worked out a plan to spice up her proposal already?

"I was serious," he warned. "I don't want a Band-Aid. You need a highly polished knock-'em-dead new angle that I can't refuse."

"I've been at it all day. Didn't even stop to eat."

That made two of them. She must be as hungry as he was, and he was starved. After a day alternating between meetings and being glued to his desk, he felt restless, too. Itchy. *Hot.* When his gaze dropped to her lips again, he ran a finger inside his steamy collar. He ought to go.

Cole eased around her. "Now isn't a good time."

"Now is a *great* time."

"I'm late."

"What for this time?"

He rotated back. "I'm sure I don't have to answer that," he said. But when he saw the disappointment shining in her eyes, his gut kicked and, against his better judgment, he found himself giving in to this infernal woman for a second time that day.

"But, if you're that keen," he muttered, heading back, "I'll give you five minutes."

"Five minutes isn't nearly enough—"

"Five minutes." He set his case on his personal assistant's desk and flicked on the desk lamp. "Starting now."

Taryn froze for three beats before setting her laptop down. When she thumbed a button, an impressive spread—com-

plete with feature banner—flashed on to the screen. Setting
his hands on his hips, Cole slanted his head. Nice effect. Although he wasn't sold on the title.

"Hot Spots?"

"We thought it had more bite than the original name."

"We?"

"Roman and me. I know it sounds kind of provocative—"

"If you want to tape an endless stream of topless bars and
nudist beaches," he cut in, "sorry, it ain't gonna fly."

The airwaves were clogged enough with that content.

"I was going to say that it's more a hook than anything
erotic. Let me show you a preliminary list of locations that
have shown interest *and,* as of today, have offered to cover
all associated costs."

The screen page flipped over to reveal a slide show of a resort Cole knew—although not personally. Only a sheik could
afford the prices. He could think of better ways to blow a million or two. Still, the cogs in his brain began to whir faster.

"That's Dubai."

When he named that country's most exclusive resort, Taryn
nodded with a grin in her eyes. "All expenses paid there. *Everything.*"

"That's impressive. But that's *one* location. I imagine you'll
do the grand tour of the resort and surrounds, which will make
good footage, but what's the twist?"

Where's the something new?

Their shoulders all but touching, she angled in more and,
in the soft shadows, those blue eyes were hypnotic. Then that
natural warmth of hers reached out again. Sumptuous. Sooth-
ing. It was like being enveloped by the lure of a toasty fire
after coming in from the cold. When his fingertips began to
tingle where they lay splayed on the desk next to hers, he was
struck by the urge to cover her hand, maybe tug her close and
see if he couldn't experience some of that warmth head-on.

Sucking down a breath, he straightened.

Definitely time to go.

"I'll think it over."

"Will you?"

He arched a brow. "What's that supposed to mean?"

"You've already made up your mind."

"If you believe that, why are you here?" *Wasting my time.*

"Because I also believe in this show." Her chin lifted. "And that wasn't five minutes."

"It was long enough." Especially considering the way he was feeling.

"But I have more to show you, Cole. Lots more."

The tendons between his shoulders, up the length of his thighs, all hardened to steel and then locked. He should get this charade over with. Tell her now. Stay on course. But how was he supposed to deal with that dewy-eyed, indignant look without feeling like the world's biggest heel?

An image of Dex's puzzle flashed into his mind's eye and something he'd thought unbending inside of him grudgingly moved. Before he could talk himself out of it, he took a mental sword and cut them both some slack. Taryn had more to show him?

"Then get your gear." He grabbed his case and headed out. "You're coming with me."

Four

When Cole Hunter insisted she accompany him to dinner, Taryn's entire body flashed hot. Time alone in that kind of setting was a bad idea. The way he sometimes looked at her—with curiosity and hunger simmering in his eyes—he might want to consume a big juicy steak but in a deeper place, whether he admitted it or not, Cole was also flipping a coin, deciding whether he could afford a side order of her.

Sorry, but she wasn't on the menu.

Then again Guthrie Hunter's son was prickly enough. The edge she rode where he and her position at Hunters was concerned was already razor thin. If she refused this "invitation," Cole might close up completely and, like it or not, after listening to Roman's stories regarding the "Commander" all day, she'd come to the conclusion that she needed Cole on her side.

Plus, her brain and body were running on empty.

Although every instinct warned against leaving this building alone with Cole, she guessed they could talk business while they ate. The golden rule, however, still applied. She had no intention of getting too close to trouble.

So, with nerves jumping in her stomach, Taryn accompanied him out, collecting her bag on the way. They passed late-shift news employees with their noses to the grindstone. Cole sent a good-night to the uniformed security man, who stood watch near the giant glass autosliders, and a moment later he was opening the passenger-side door of a low-slung Italian sports car. Taryn's throat bobbed on an involuntary swallow. She had the weirdest feeling if she crawled inside that dark warm space, she might never come out.

Soon they were buckled up and weaving through Sydney's upper-end streets. In the near distance, arcing lights from the bridge spread shimmering silver ribbons over the harbor while beside her Cole changed gears with the intuitive grace of a professional. She couldn't ignore that subtle yet intoxicating masculine scent, the ease with which his large tanned hands gripped the leather of the wheel. In such close proximity, his legs seemed somehow too long, those shoulders almost too broad. Every available inch of this car seemed *filled* with the smoldering energy that was Cole Hunter.

Taryn pressed back into the molded bucket seat and clenched her hands in her lap. She'd never felt more unsettled. Never more female.

As they flew over a main arterial and the busy world whirred by, he said, "I'd kill for a good thick steak."

"I thought you'd be a steak man."

"You're not a steak woman?"

"Vegetarian."

"I'm sure my regular place caters for that."

"You mean caters for those of us who choose to live on the fringes."

In the rapid-fire shadows, his crooked grin flashed white. "No disrespect intended. I grew up in a male-dominated household. Tofu and soy weren't in our vocabulary."

Taryn peered out the window. She didn't care about Cole's eating habits. She cared only about getting this proposal through and at last moving forward with this show.

"Guess we're all products of our childhood," she offered absently.

"What about you?"

"What about me?"

"Lots of brothers and sisters?"

"I'm an only child."

His deep rich chuckle resonated around the car cabin, burrowing into her skin, seeping into her bones.

"You must have had a peaceful time growing up," he said.

Peaceful? "I guess you could call it that."

"What would you call it?"

That was easy.

"Lonely."

His hand on the gearshift, he hesitated changing down before he double-clutched then wove into the lit circular drive of an establishment that smacked of class and exorbitant prices. A uniformed man strode over to see to her door before a valet parked the car. They entered through open, white-paneled doors into an area decorated in swirls of bronze and planes of muted cherry-red. The large room's lighting was soft. Inviting.

Way too intimate.

While Taryn tried to concentrate on the weight of her laptop in her carryall over her shoulder rather than Cole's strong chiseled profile, from behind the front desk, the maître d' tipped his head.

"I'm afraid we weren't expecting you this evening, Mr. Hunter. Your regular table isn't available." The older man's attention slid to her and his helpful smile deepened. "We do, however, have a private balcony setting with a magnificent view of the harbor."

"Sounds good." Cole rapped his fingertips on the leather-bound menu lying on the counter. "And, er, Marco, you have vegetarian dishes here, right?"

Marco didn't blink. "We have a wide selection. Our chef will also be happy to accommodate any particular requests."

As Marco escorted them to that private balcony, Taryn swore she felt heat radiating from Cole's hand where she imagined it rested inches from the small of her back. Then, when they slipped through into a curtained-off area, her breath hitched in her throat. The mixture of lilting music and silver moonlight, along with her striking company for the evening…she felt as if she'd stepped into a dream. She'd been out to dinner with attractive men at fine restaurants before, but this scene—this surreal heady feeling—was something else.

Retracting an upholstered bergère chair for her, Marco asked, "A wine menu this evening, Mr. Hunter?"

Cole rattled off the name of a vintage that Marco's widening eyes hinted was exceptional. A moment later, the curtain was drawn and they were once again completely alone.

Enjoying the atmosphere despite herself, Taryn shifted in the chair, which was more comfortable than her sofa. "I wasn't expecting this."

"You'd prefer an all-you-can-eat salad bar?"

With delicious aromas filling the air, her taste buds had already decided. She opened the menu. "Here will do nicely."

And every one of those dishes listed without prices sounded divine. Still, she would keep in the forefront of her mind that this was not an occasion to forget herself. In fact, she might as well put this idle time to good use.

Having chosen her meal, she set her menu aside and extracted her laptop from her carryall. With a grunt of disapproval, Cole sat back.

"We won't do that now."

"I'd rather get to it before you have a drink or two."

"I can assure you a couple of glasses of wine won't affect my judgment." His lips twitched. "You, of course, may be a different matter."

"I'm not a giggler, Mr. Hunter."

His frown returned. "And ditch the Mr. this and manners that. My name's Cole. You call my father Guthrie, don't you?"

"That's different. We're on friendly terms."

"Really? Did *he* take you out to dinner?"

She almost gasped. She knew what he was implying. "Of course not."

"Maybe *you* took him."

She slanted her head. "You won't put me off—*Cole*. If you want me gone from Hunters, you'll have to drag me out, kicking and screaming."

"Is that what happened at your last job?"

On the tabletop her fists curled. What would she bet he already knew?

At that moment, Marco arrived to serve wine and take orders, giving Taryn time enough to sort out her answer—and her temper. With Marco having left through the curtains again, she admitted, "I was let go from my last position."

Wineglass midway to his mouth, Cole stopped. "Didn't get along with your boss?"

"We got along great."

"Ah." He sipped, swallowed. "I see."

She burned to set him straight, and in the bluntest of terms, but she wouldn't give him the satisfaction.

"Upper management made the decision," she said. "My direct boss was always good to me. Very much a father figure."

"Seems you're partial to them. Don't you have one of your own?"

"A father?" Taking a long cool sip of water, she swallowed past the pit in her throat. "As a matter of fact, I don't."

Cole's shoulders seemed to lock before he set down his wineglass and said in a lower tone, "We were talking about your previous employ."

She explained about ending up the scapegoat for leaked in-

formation regarding those series ideas. Her plan had been to
keep her story brief but Cole had a question for everything.
He was quite the interrogator. Thorough and emotionless, as
Roman had warned. Finally satisfied on that particular subject, he nodded.

"But you've landed on your feet," he offered, finger-
combing back a dark lock blown over his brow by a harbor
breeze.

"Seems that will depend on you."

"Or, rather, what you've got for me."

At that moment, their meals arrived and Cole took the lib-
erty of refilling her wineglass. She hadn't realized she'd almost drained it.

"But I'm too damn hungry to focus," he said, setting the
wine back down. "Let's eat."

While they enjoyed their meals, small talk was difficult to
avoid—general topics at first…the state of the industry, current affairs. When he asked, she let him know that Guthrie's
personal assistant had rung to apologize that regrettably he
wouldn't have time to welcome her into their fold properly that
day. Then conversation swerved toward lighter subject matter
about schools and interests growing up. Cole had served in the
Navy Cadets with a friend who owned his own security firm
now. He said that once he'd even wanted to become a high-
seas officer. She'd grinned at that. Who would have guessed?

Cole changed the tone and the subject back to family. Almost finished with their meals, he spoke about his mother—
just a few words, but they were said with such sincerity and
affection, Taryn felt moved. More than instinct said that this
was a side of Cole others would rarely see. His next question
was obvious, and yet she'd been so caught up in ingesting this
small taste of "human Cole" that she hadn't seen it coming.

"Most daughters are close to their mothers," he said. "Does
yours live nearby? In town?"

Taryn's stomach jumped but she forced the emotion down. She'd lived with the reality all her life. Woke up to it every morning. And still that empty sick feeling rose in a surge whenever she needed to say the words aloud.

She set down her fork. "My mother's dead."

His brows nudged together and he took a moment before responding.

"I'm sorry."

Yeah. Where her mother was concerned, she was sorry about a lot of things.

But this wasn't a first date. They weren't here to analyze the past—how some were born to rule while others were left to build on crumbs. Still, the evening hadn't been the disaster she'd half expected, although now was the time to gently but firmly reset some boundaries.

"I'd rather not discuss my personal life."

"Sure." He nodded. "I understand. I was only making conversation—"

"I know, Cole. That's fine." She pushed down those rising levels again and pasted on a reasonable face. "But we're here because you wanted to eat. Let's get that out of the way so we can get back to work."

While Taryn set about consuming the remainder of her salad, Cole warred with himself. He understood this occasion was in no way a catch-up between friends or, God forbid, a night out for lovers. He had indeed been making polite conversation—and he'd ended up sticking his foot in his mouth once again. He knew about the pain of losing a parent, but how was he to know that Taryn had lost both a father *and* a mother?

Yes, best they keep any subsequent talk firmly centered on business, he decided, draining his glass. Definitely best they conduct future meetings in a work environment—*if* Taryn and her proposal made it past this evening.

One glass of wine, half a steak and no conversation later, Cole set his napkin firmly down on the table beside his plate.

"Okay. We're done. Let's talk." And get back to our own lives.

Finished, too, Taryn slid her plate aside, collected her laptop and scooted her chair slightly toward his, purely to offer a better view of the screen. Before the hard drive had finished booting up, she'd outlined logistics on travel points and was expounding on visions for the future. But he was done with being chatty. Now he wanted the heart of her revised idea, and he wanted it fast.

"What's the hook?" he asked. "The draw card that'll have everyone and their great-grandma tuning back in week after week and advertisers cuing up?"

A manicured fingertip brushed a key and an image flashed up on the screen…a rather uninspiring shot of a group of people standing in an ordinary suburban front yard. The way Taryn was beaming, you'd think she was about to Skype with the person at the top of her "must meet" list.

Cole loosened his tie. God, why had he bothered? Why was he bothering *still*?

"Rather than trained reporters," she said, moving to the next image—a handful of kids playing basketball in some run-down hall, "we'll use real-life couples or families or groups to check out each holiday hot spot. We'll ask viewers to email or text in reasons why they, or someone they know, ought to be the next to enjoy an all-expenses-paid trip to some amazing place, courtesy of Hunters."

He barely contained a groan. "This is another reality show idea, isn't it?"

"Reality shows are still extremely popular," she insisted, rolling through more similarly uninspiring images, "and with this formula—coupling luxury with underprivileged—we can truly tug at the heartstrings of our viewers." When he groaned aloud, she tipped toward him. "Open up your mind to the possibilities and all the people you could help make happy."

"I'm not here to organize charities. I'm here to make good television." Make money.

She blinked then returned her attention to the screen and went on.

"At the end of the season, the viewers get to vote on the number-one holiday couple, family, friends or whatever, and the main sponsor donates a potful of cash toward helping an associated community cause. The next season kicks off with a lucky draw winner from a list of all the voters."

She looked so animated—her big eyes twinkling and hands dancing—he practically saw sparks fly. But…

"It's not new enough," he said. When she looked at him, puzzled, he elaborated. "I need more. Maybe if you include some sort of elimination strategy—"

"*No.* I want everyone associated with my show to feel like winners."

He pinched the bridge of his nose. Great. He was dealing with an I-can-save-the-world type. Not that philanthropy wasn't admirable. In this instance, however, it simply wasn't feasible. He'd grown up living and breathing the culture of broadcasting. He'd learned from the best, and now, he delivered the same. Or wanted to. He didn't know why Guthrie had let this stunt get as far as it had, but in the morning he'd tell his father he should consider a vacation. In fact, a lengthy holiday away from business—and would-be assassins—sounded like a damn fine idea.

"This will be a feel-good program," she was saying. "Sure, along the way there'll be all sorts of trials and fears faced, but no one will be left feeling like a loser. This show could start a whole new genre."

"Taryn," he said gently but clearly, "there is no show unless I say so."

She tacked up her slipping smile. "Think of the sponsors."

"You can talk all you want about sponsor dollars, but in the end time is money. My time. The company's time. I won't put valuable people on a project I'm not convinced will succeed."

"Not convinced *yet*," she corrected.

Blast it all. She wasn't listening.

"You shouldn't have rushed this. You should have given yourself at *least* a couple of days to really think through every possible angle."

"My idea was good to begin with."

He sucked down a breath. Okay. Blunt ax time. "There's no room at Hunters for *good*. I'm after brilliant—or nothing."

"Brilliant?"

"That's right."

Her gaze hardened. Then it turned to stone. "Because you're so brilliant?"

"Because, I'm the *boss* and—" *dammit* "—no one gets to play in my sandbox unless I say so."

Her eyes filled with an emotion that glistened at the same time as it burned. Then her hands fisted an instant before she pushed out of her chair. On her way up, she bumped the table and her glass toppled toward him. Wine hurled through the air, ending up with a splash on his lap. His arms flew out; at the same time his temper spiked and he slid his chair back. Was that an accident or was she deliberately making matters worse?

Still in his seat, Cole gripped his napkin and pressed at the cool alcohol seeping into his trousers. Somehow he managed to keep his voice even.

"I'll assume that was an accident."

"It was." She leaned across the table and flung the wine from his glass, too. "That one, I *did* mean."

Five

She shouldn't have done it.

God knows, she ought to have kept her head and tried to contain the smoke rather than flinging more fuel on the fire. But as Taryn stormed out through the five-star restaurant, half-aware of curious patrons' heads turning, that more volatile side of her nature was glad she'd let Cole Hunter know precisely what she'd thought. Sandbox, indeed!

He was lucky a glass of wine was all she'd thrown.

Outside, the fresh air hit. Stopping at the bottom of the restaurant's half-dozen stone steps, she glanced around with stinging eyes before the realization struck. Cole had driven her here. To collect her sedan, she'd need to grab a cab back to Hunters.

And tomorrow? Cole had as good as said her idea sucked and she was through. Hopefully Guthrie would have something to say about that. But if she went to the senior Hunter about this situation, she'd feel like a tattletale whining to daddy about her bullying big brother. How she longed to circle her hands around Cole's big tanned neck and squeeze until he turned blue. Lord how she wished she'd never met the man.

She noticed a concerned-looking doorman crossing over at

the same time a low, smooth voice wrapped around to startle and disarm her from behind.

"Would you kindly tell me what that was about?"

She swung around and glared into Cole Hunter's flashing green eyes. She hated that her voice was shaky.

"Kindly leave me alone."

"You came with me—"

"And I'll leave without you." She directed her next words to the fidgety doorman. "Can you organize a cab, please?"

Waving a hand, Cole sent the poor doorman back to his corner. "I'll drive you to the station, or home, if you like."

"I'd prefer you didn't."

"I'd prefer that I did."

"So you can goad me into doing something else I might regret?"

He stepped closer until his shadow consumed her and his lidded gaze dropped to her lips. "And just what is it you're afraid you'll do?"

When his eyes met hers again, she felt the stakes between them change and swell. Was it her imagination or had he just propositioned her?

She ought to be outraged. She should want to slap his face. But the heat racing over her skin, snatching her breath and warming her insides, suddenly felt less like anger and a whole lot more like anticipation.

She croaked out, "I never asked to come here tonight."

"No. You were only jumping around like a Christmas puppy, wanting me to see your idea right away."

"You said you wanted to see it."

"When it was good and cooked."

She hitched her carryall strap higher on her shoulder. "Admit it. You never had any intention of giving me a chance."

"*Whoa.* Don't put this back on me."

"No. I should be overjoyed with needing to jump through your hoops after I've already landed the job."

He blinked at that then absently readjusted the platinum watchband on his wrist. "I'm yet to speak to my father about signing you without consulting me first."

"Perhaps you should have done that before putting me through that charade."

"Sorry for doing you a favor."

"Forgive me if I don't shower you with thanks."

A cab rolled up the lantern-lit drive while a valet brought Cole's car around at the same time. Shaking with rage—with hurt and frustration—she made a beeline for the cab with Cole hot on her tail.

That doorman came forward to open the passenger door. With one sharp look, Cole sent him packing again. Then, refocusing, he crossed his arms over that stained damp shirt.

"I'm sorry you can't handle the truth about the premise of your show."

"*Your* version of the truth," she pointed out.

"Like it or not, mine's the only version that counts."

She crossed her arms, too. "Has anyone ever suggested that your ego might be a trifle oversize?"

"My temper, too—particularly, but not excluding, when I'm soaked through and smelling like a barroom floor."

Her conscience pricked. She looked him up and down. Then, although it pained, she offered up what her aunt might consider polite and fair.

"I'll pay for dry cleaning."

"Shirt, trousers and tie." He pretended to wring the strip of royal-blue silk. "You didn't miss much."

"There's nothing wrong with my pitching arm. I was captain of my school softball team five years running."

"Remind me to stay out of your way if you try to swing a bat."

"Don't worry. I'll make sure none of my home runs land in your sandbox."

Cole looked at her harder, his gaze penetrating—judgmental—and yet she got the impression that a different, less hostile emotion churned just below his surface. Maybe a miniscule touch of grudging respect? She crossed her arms tighter. *Too little, too late.*

Finally he shrugged back both shoulders and tucked in his chin. "Maybe I was a little over-the-top with the sandbox line."

She pretended to tug her ear. "Was that Cole Hunter *apologizing?*"

"Merely an observation."

His brows lifted as if he were waiting for her to return the sentiment. No way would she give another inch.

Except...

She didn't need for Cole to walk away from this confrontation thinking he was the better man. She might be right, but she wasn't stupid.

With the cabbie and doorman hanging back, waiting, she eased out that pent-up breath and let her arms unravel.

"Well, maybe," she ground out, "I didn't need to toss that second drink over your lap."

The intensity of his gaze gradually lifted and, after another deliberative moment, he tilted his head at his car. "So you up for a lift back to the station?"

"Only if I choose the topic of conversation."

He clutched at his chest. "You'll even *talk* to me?"

"Not about anything personal. And I'd prefer not to discuss my project with you any more at this time."

"I'm sure that's wise." He started off then stopped, waiting for her to join him, which—after making him stand there wondering for another five full beats—she did.

"Maybe we could discuss vegetarian cuisine," she said as they reached his car.

He grunted. "What about sports?"

"I'm in charge, remember?"

After she'd slid in, but before he shut the door, she heard him mutter, "Enjoy it while it lasts."

Cole drove back to the station listening to Taryn share her secrets on the abundance of ways one could combine pumpkin with pine nuts. Fascinating.

But now, as he made his third stop for the evening—at his father's Pott's Point mansion—he could admit he'd almost enjoyed the final stint of his evening with this persistent producer. Even as the wine dried on his clothes, he surrendered a smile remembering the poised timbre of her voice and glorious lines of her legs as she'd chatted on.

One moment spitting fire, the next a consummate ice queen. He didn't know which intrigued him more. From the moment he'd laid eyes on her, sitting demurely in his father's reception lounge, he'd been struck by those lips, her hair, that barely subdued sexuality. After her spectacular meltdown at the restaurant tonight, perverse though it might sound, his attraction for her had only grown.

By the time he pulled up beneath his father's extravagant granite forecourt, Cole was trying to shake the image of Taryn twining her arms around his neck and searching out his kiss—not because he felt guilty necessarily, but because he didn't need any added aggravation when he visited this place. Guthrie he could handle. His father's wife, Cole didn't want to touch.

He'd fortified himself and was about to slip out of the car when his cell sounded. Two callers—Dex and Wynn combined. Cole connected and Wynn spoke first.

"How's Dad holding up?"

Then Dex. "Do the authorities have any clue who's behind it all?"

"We'll get the guy," Cole told them. "Don't worry."

Cole hadn't been able to get a hold of either brother this morning, or Teagan, for that matter. They had their differences but, beyond and above all else, they were a family. Cole wasn't certain which brother had organized this conference call, but he was grateful to have the opportunity to fill them in. Dex and Wynn had a right, an *obligation,* to know about this second attempt on their father's life, and Guthrie would never tell them. He wouldn't want any of his children to worry.

When Cole finished passing on the incident's details, Wynn cursed under his breath.

"Cole, what's the plan? You'll put some safety measures in place, right? Get a P.I. on board?"

Dex's deep laugh rumbled down the line. "As if Cole could stop himself from taking charge."

Cole huffed. "I don't hear either of you offering to fly back and help man the fort."

"As a matter of fact—" Wynn started at the same time Dex said, "I'll be right out—"

But Cole cut them both off. "Stay where you are." Wynn couldn't spare time away from his seat in New York and Dex's smugness would only drive his older brother nuts. "I can handle whatever has to be done."

Dex said, "Well, if you need anything…"

Flicking a glance toward the house, Cole thought of his stepmother. "Maybe a leash," he muttered.

Wynn asked, "What was that?"

"Nothing." Cole opened the car door. "I'll keep you guys in the loop." He hung up, and a moment later rang the bell. A woman he'd never seen before fanned open the tall timber door. His expression must have looked as confused as hers. Drab, overweight. Was that a mustache? Shrinking back, he thrust his hands into his pockets.

"Who the devil are you?"

"I work for the Hunters."

Cole examined the woman's garb: a dreary gray old-fashioned uniform. "What happened to Silvia?" And her vibrant colors and big friendly smile.

The woman shrugged a pair of round shoulders. "Think the madam said she'd been here too long."

He grunted. Obviously Silvia had become an annoyance for dear Eloise. He'd seen the calculating look in the younger woman's eye whenever the Hunters' much-loved housekeeper had entered a room or dared to have a laugh with Guthrie. Silvia knew this house, the history and its characters inside and out. And like the Hunter boys, Silvia hadn't approved of the master's new bride one scrap. Seemed it'd taken Eloise five years to weed their old friend out. So, who was next on the ambitious second Mrs. Hunter's hit list?

The new help wiped a worn hand down her starched apron and asked, "Who shall I say is calling?"

"Name's Cole."

Dull hazel eyes rounded. "Mr. Hunter's eldest?"

As she studied the wine drying on his shirt, he wove around her. "Where can I find him?"

In the cavernous double-story foyer, another voice joined in. One Cole recognized—and loathed.

"Cole, honey, come on through."

Decked out in a full-length silk robe the color of ripe strawberries, Eloise beckoned him from beneath the decorative arch that led into the front sitting room. He wondered if she were vain enough to wear all that makeup to bed. So different from his naturally beautiful mother. He wouldn't start on the difference between poise and class.

Dismissing the stirring in the pit of his gut, Cole strode forward. "I wanted to check in and see how he was doing."

"After that terrible business this morning, you mean."

Cole was already inside and glancing around that sitting

room. An *empty* room. He ran a hand through his hair. He really didn't have time for hide-and-seek.

"Where is he?"

He spun around. Eloise was standing so close behind, he almost knocked her over. Theatrical, as usual, she emitted a small cry of surprise and swayed, no doubt hoping he'd physically prevent her fall.

Cole only stepped well back then asked, "Is he in the study?"

Filing long graceful fingers back through her disrupted fire-red mane, Eloise pretended to gather herself before heading for the liquor cabinet and holding up a decanter.

"Can I tempt you?"

Cole shuddered. *Not on your life.*

He made a civil excuse. "I'm tight on time."

Examining his shirt, she set down the decanter and strolled back over. "Looks like you've already indulged."

"My father, Eloise. Where is he?"

"Your father's not here. He went out with that new bodyguard of his." Looking inward, she frowned. "Tall. Brooding. Not a friendly type at all."

Cole grinned. *Good.* Last thing Guthrie needed was the man meant to protect him succumbing to the mistress's so-called charm.

Retrieving his cell, Cole speed dialed his father. When Guthrie didn't pick up, Cole left a text message: Call CH ASAP. Then he headed for the door, muttering to Eloise on his way out, "I won't keep you."

But, in her sweeping strawberry robe, she was already scooting around him like her rear end was on fire. When she faced him again, a generous amount of cleavage was showing. Guthrie said she made him happy, and Cole could imagine Eloise doing just about anything to maintain her allowance.

Then again, if her older husband was out of the picture, she wouldn't have to please anyone but herself.

"Before you go, I was hoping you could help me out," she was saying. "Or rather help your little brother."

About to push on around her, Cole stopped. Dates indicated that Guthrie had married Eloise when she was already pregnant with a boy the whole family had instantly taken into their hearts. Whenever Cole visited, his little brother would talk about becoming a fireman, or, if he wasn't brave enough for that, one of Santa's elves. Oh, to be that innocent.

Cole asked, "What's Tate want?"

Eloise collected an electronic gadget off a nearby sideboard. "Tate was a horror this evening when he couldn't get this to work. I had to send him to bed early."

Cole almost reached for the children's e-tablet then thought better of it. He wanted to help, but it was wiser to leave.

"Dad can fix it when he gets home."

She laughed. "You're funny. Your father working something like this out."

Cole scowled. "He's an intelligent man."

"But, honey, he isn't a *young* man." Her gaze stroked the expanse of his chest. "What we need here is someone who's up-to-date with all the latest." She held the gadget out again. "Tate will be so proud when I tell him big brother Cole took the time to fix this."

Cole set his jaw. He had no time for Eloise, but he loved Tate. Cole pitied him too for having a mother who placed the importance of painting her nails above anything her son might like to share. Last Christmas, while Tate had ripped open his presents and pored over the bike and Rollerblades Santa had left, Eloise had been a big no-show. When she'd finally scraped herself out of bed around noon, bloodshot eyes told the story of a boozy Christmas Eve. At the time Cole had wondered with whom. His father had looked fit enough to run a marathon, even if he didn't quite meet his eldest son's unimpressed gaze.

Reminding himself to think only of Tate, Cole took the device and perused the program keys. When, pretending to be curious, Eloise and her claws tipped too close for comfort, Cole lifted his gaze and issued a pointed look. *Back off.* At the same time, he caught movement near the archway. That woman—the new housekeeper—stood halfway hidden behind the connecting wall. Eloise followed Cole's line of vision and, taken aback, drew her robe's opening shut.

"Nancy, you go on to your quarters," Eloise said. "I won't be needing you anymore tonight."

With a curt nod, Nancy and her mustache slunk away. If Eloise wanted female help that her husband would find not the least attractive, she'd creamed the top shelf. And Cole didn't restrict that to looks. Nancy was downright creepy.

Attention on the tablet again, Cole fiddled until the screen lit up. After making certain the applications worked, he slid the device back on the sideboard. As he headed out through the foyer, a disappointed Eloise called out in her annoying Southern drawl.

"Your daddy will be back soon. Sure you don't want to stay awhile?"

Cole opened the door and kept right on walking.

Taryn Quinn didn't like to discuss family. He didn't particularly like discussing his, either. An out-of-control playboy brother, a big bad stepmom and a father someone wanted dead.

As Cole slid back into his car then ignited the turbo engine, he wondered again who was the mastermind behind the bullets this morning. His father was absent tonight. Did that mean this bodyguard he'd hired was on someone's trail? When this ugly situation was done with and the perpetrator behind prison bars, he'd certainly sleep a lot better. But for now…

It was late and he was sticky.

Keeping the revs down so as not to wake Tate, he rolled down the drive as his thoughts swung again to Taryn Quinn. She'd denied any romantic connections with her former boss and he believed her. But a woman like Ms. Quinn wasn't long without an intimate relationship, and after witnessing the fiery side of her nature tonight, it'd be easier if the terms "Taryn Quinn" and "supersexy" weren't tangled up together in his head.

Accelerating, Cole swung onto the wide tree-lined Pott's Point road and wondered. Was Taryn "taken" or was she "taking a break"? Could be she was a new age woman who, too busy for connections, preferred the advantages of a friend with benefits. If he wasn't certain she'd hurl something heavy at his head, he'd set aside his business-only-with-employees rule and ask.

Giving in to a grin, he shot onto the expressway.

Hell, he just might ask anyway.

Six

"Thought I'd warn you. The boss is on the warpath."

Yanked from her thoughts by that familiar Brit voice, Taryn glanced up to find Roman Lyons poking his head into her office. She lowered her pen to her desk.

"Guthrie?"

"No. The *younger* Mr. Hunter. Grapevine says he's headed this way."

Sending a fortifying wink, Rowan bowed off for the relative safety of his own office while, holding her swooping stomach, Taryn siphoned down a breath.

Remarkably, after the wine incident last night, she and Cole had parted on amicable terms. Back here to collect her car, once again she'd offered to pay his laundry bill. Cole had declined then had said in a low sure voice that they'd talk more tomorrow. Well, tomorrow was here and, unlike her normal self, Taryn was positively shaky.

Discussing recipes on the drive back from the restaurant, she'd given the impression that she'd regained her customary cool, but remaining composed whenever Cole Hunter was around was more difficult than killing a blaze with a thimble of water. She'd barely slept for planning how best to handle this, their next meeting. Tossing and turning, she'd imagined a score of different scenarios, and each dreamed-up conversation had included her witty but also *upbeat* remarks. She'd decided. She wasn't throwing in the towel just yet.

Now every one of those let's-try-to-get-along phrases flew like buckshot from her mind as Cole's larger-than-life self strode into the room. This morning he looked broader, darker and, dammit, *hotter* than any man had a right…like an almighty tropical storm rolling in from the sea. Pressing back into her chair, Taryn quivered and spoke before she thought.

"You're always doing that."

"Doing what?"

"Thundering around."

The black slashes of his brows hiked up. "Well, good morning to you, too."

Taryn bit her lip to stop from telling him not to look at her that way—as if *she* was hard work when, in fact, she only wanted to get along and move forward. But, no matter how he pressed her buttons—and he seemed to press every one—her survival here at Hunters depended on making a monumental effort. Which meant reclaiming her biggest asset—her poise—and being hospitable as well as professional. In other words, she needed to present herself the way she would in any person's company other than the Commander's.

Willing her locked muscles to relax, Taryn resumed her calm and asked, "Have you had breakfast?" She reached for a food container, which waited strategically on her desk, and pried back the plastic lid. "Scones," she told him. "Homemade fresh this morning."

Curious, he craned to see. "Is there pumpkin involved?"

"But no pine nuts." She found her feet. "I was about to pour a coffee. Want one? I brought in my own percolator. I'm more your slow, full, satisfying type than an instant kind of girl."

"Slow and satisfying. Who'd have guessed?"

On her way to the percolator, she stopped and caught his look. But her comment wasn't meant to be provocative. She'd been talking about hot drinks, for God's sake, not sex. Before she could qualify or downplay her remark, Cole went on.

"So you've made yourself at home," he said, looking around.

She burned to say, *And why not?* This was her office until Guthrie said otherwise. Which reminded her.

She lifted the pot. "Have you spoken to your father yet?"

"I haven't been able to track him down this morning."

"He's off the station?"

"I have no idea where he is."

China cup full, she glanced over and was taken aback. Cole's assured expression had been replaced by a mask of worry. She hadn't thought he had any vulnerabilities, or none that he'd be prepared to show. Maybe it was inappropriate, but she wanted to ask him what was wrong.

But then that expression evaporated and, drawing himself up tall, he told her, "No coffee, thanks. And no scones."

Before he could say anything more—like, for instance, "I'm only here to tell you to pack your stuff and shove off"—Taryn revved her "perfect employee" enthusiasm back up to high.

"I've been going through my notes again, making phone calls. I'd like to do a full survey of *Hot Spots'* first destination."

"Why would I approve a survey when I haven't approved the show?"

"Because you have nothing to lose. I'll pay for airfares. Accommodation is sorted, no cost."

"And who do you propose to take along with you on this survey—*if* I approve?"

"I don't need anyone else. I know what to look for in locations and angles."

"Wouldn't it be prudent to take a cameraman so I could look over footage later? If—"

"If you approve," she finished before he could. She didn't need reminding again. "If it's a deal-breaker, I'll pay for a co-worker's fare, as well."

"Of course, it could save time and trouble if I simply came along and checked out the location for myself."

Taryn's heart jumped to her throat and then she remembered to breathe. But of course, with that menacing smile playing around the corners of his lips, Cole was only testing. Wanting her to rear up and give him a reason to be even more negative. He could toss on all the heat he could muster. She would neither wither into a quivering mess nor self-combust with indignation. She refused to let him get under her skin like he had last night.

Rather, she called his bluff.

"Sure." She wound her arms over her high-waisted black skirt and pegged out a leg. "If you want to come along, why not?"

His gaze sharpened. "You want me to go?"

"It was your suggestion."

Cole felt his grin grow. One thing he could say for Taryn Quinn—she wasn't a quitter. She had her teeth in here and she'd do anything not to let go. Of course, there would be no survey because, after her rushed effort last night, as soon as he got it straight with his father, Taryn's contract would be terminated and she'd be out the door. Business was business. His objective was to keep Hunter Broadcasting healthy—afloat and viable—even if he didn't always feel like a hero doing it.

His phone sounded with a message. Guthrie was in and wanted to see him straightaway. Cole wanted to see Guthrie, too, about Taryn but also for a catch-up regarding the most recent murder attempt. He'd been worried when Guthrie hadn't been home last night. More worried still when he hadn't been in the office this morning. He'd left messages but had gotten no reply.

He slotted his phone away and headed out. "We'll talk more about this later."

She sang back, "I'll be here."

Leaving Taryn, he headed for his father's office. Midway down that long connecting corridor, Cole noticed two assistant producers deep in conversation. He heard Taryn's name mentioned before they saw him. Talk ceased and they ducked off down an adjoining hall.

Everyone here knew belts were drawn tight. Most would also know about his lack of interest in certain types of shows and that the new kid on the block was touting just that kind of proposal. She might have gotten past Guthrie, but Cole wouldn't be surprised if bets were on, speculating on how soon her ax would fall. He hoped Taryn's ears weren't burning.

When he entered his father's office, Guthrie was sitting behind his desk, studying a spreadsheet. At the far end of the room, a tall, suited man Cole had never met before took in the harbor views. As the man turned to face him, Guthrie moved from behind his desk to the more casual area of his office. At a circle of tub chairs, Guthrie took a seat and introduced Cole to Jeremy Judge, his personal bodyguard.

Eyes on the stony-faced man, who was a private investigator as well, Cole folded down into the chair alongside his father's.

"Please take a seat, Mr. Judge."

Judge sent Cole a thin-lipped smile. "I spend too much time sitting around. In cars. Park benches. Surveillance work, you know. I prefer to stretch my back when I can."

No mistaking—Jeremy Judge had a vigilant air. Cole wasn't sure he'd blinked once.

Looking relieved but weary, Guthrie crossed his legs. "I'm

happy to say Jeremy has successfully tracked down the man responsible for the attempts on my life."

Cole sat straighter. Well, that was fast. "I hope he's under arrest."

"Last time I saw," Judge said, "he was under a car. While I was escorting your father home around seven, we were fired upon."

"I'd dropped in to see your uncle," Guthrie explained.

"Uncle Talbot?" His father's older brother? "I can't remember the last time you 'dropped in' on him."

The brothers hadn't spoken in years. Cole wasn't even sure what the problem was about anymore.

"We're different as chalk and cheese, but when we were younger, Talbot and I were close," Guthrie said. "I felt the need to catch up."

Cole absorbed his father's words. When someone's life was in danger, guess they'd feel compelled to sort out past differences with people who should matter…just in case.

"As Mr. Hunter moved to enter the car, two shots rang out," Judge said. "I pursued the gunman on foot. He panicked and ran in front of traffic."

Cole sized up Judge, and the situation. "A rather clumsy assassin, wouldn't you say?"

"Clearly," Judge said, "he didn't anticipate the chase."

"Which hospital was he taken to?" Cole asked.

"Head injuries were extensive," Judge said. "He died before paramedics got to the scene."

Cole cleared the sudden blockage in his throat. Had he heard right? Just like that, the guy had been creamed and this god-awful drama was over?

But of course this episode was far from finished. A stack of questions needed answers. The most obvious—why? Again Cole spoke to Judge.

"I suppose now your work truly begins."

"To dig into his background, the motives, whether he worked alone." Jeremy Judge nodded his long chin. "My first priority's to obtain the police report."

"We'll need a lawyer."

"It's cut-and-dried, son," Guthrie said.

Cole rapped his knuckles on the chair arm. He wanted to believe this problem was over. But this all seemed too quick. Too neat. And yet Judge looked so assured and his father so relieved. Hell, maybe he was too close to this situation to see this ending as the blessing it truly was. Still, he'd feel a whole lot better when this would-be killer's motives were revealed. No reason he shouldn't bring in the reserves.

Brandon was contacting him today regarding the Eloise tail, which he wouldn't call off just yet. And no reason Brandon shouldn't help Judge mop up.

"A good friend owns a security firm," Cole told Judge, reaching to find his wallet and a card. "I'll give him a call, you two can team up and—"

Guthrie cut in. "No need. Jeremy has this under control."

Judge's lips peeled back in a got-this-covered smile before he headed for the door. "I'll be in touch, sir. Good meeting you, Cole."

When Judge had left the room, Guthrie exhaled. "I can't describe the weight lifted. When you get to my age, you don't need those kinds of troubles."

Having someone hunting you down would not be pleasant. Thank God, he didn't know about his wife's antics. That'd kill him for sure.

Guthrie dabbed his forehead with a handkerchief. "Now on to more pleasant matters." He slotted the cloth away. "How are you and our new producer getting along? Moving forward?"

Cole hesitated. He wanted to give it to his father straight. He still wasn't good with Guthrie hiring Taryn Quinn without passing it by him first. Investment in any show was a huge commitment. Only surefire hits got the green light to go into production. Given the overseas hiccups—the strain on Hunter's reputation thanks to Dex's escapades and Wynn missing some plum opportunities—big brother had to watch the bottom line more closely than ever before.

But Cole swallowed the words. He imagined Taryn's big hopeful eyes then drank in his father's relaxed face again and his stomach muscles kicked.

"Taryn and I have been…talking," Cole finally said.

Leaning across, Guthrie clasped his son's forearm. "I should have consulted with you first. You know I value your opinion above all others. But I like this lady's style and I wanted to nab her before anyone else could. I have a good feeling about this." Guthrie pushed to his feet, looking taller—and stronger—than he had in weeks. "Keep me in the loop."

Cole left his father's office battling a mix of emotions. He was glad that murderous SOB who'd been trailing Guthrie was out of commission—if, indeed, that was the end of it. As far as Guthrie's opinion of Taryn Quinn and her show were concerned… Cole loved to see his father happy, but could he go against instinct and give Taryn's show a bit more rope? In the long run, cutting her free now would be kinder. He couldn't afford to spend good time and money on a project he didn't believe in, even if the producer herself intrigued him. It simply didn't make good business sense.

Down the corridor those assistant producers were back, clustered at the watercooler. Four others had joined them. They were so deep in conversation, no one saw him coming. Drawing closer, he overheard snippets:

"…haven't bothered to introduce myself."

"Bet she'll cry when he terminates…"

"…heard she's coming on to him now. Sucking up bigtime."

There were few secrets in this building. Cole Hunter had

his hatchet out. Taryn Quinn's days were numbered. Logic said why waste time getting to know a newbie when she'd be history next week anyway?

That half dozen at the cooler spotted Taryn moving from her office down the corridor. She sent them a friendly smile. When all but two looked away, pretending not to see, Cole's chest squeezed and the back of his neck went hot. Then the mob saw the boss strolling toward them. Women's eyes rounded, men cleared their throats, and one or two muttered a hasty hello.

Cole strode right past and up to Taryn. Loud enough for all to hear, he asked, "When are you booking this location survey?"

Taryn looked sideways, as if he might be drunk or fevered. Then she shook herself and replied.

"I was thinking weekend after this."

Feeling six pairs of eyes and ears upon them, Cole nodded. "Sort out expenses with accounts."

Taryn took a few seconds to respond with a shaky smile. "Sure. I'll do it straightaway."

"That's expenses for *two*."

"A cameraman?"

"You and me."

Some of the color drained from her cheeks. "You really want to go?"

His reply was a curt nod. Then he headed off toward his office, but at a reduced pace. He wanted to hear the introductions as Taryn met with that watercooler crowd. There was even a smattering of laughter.

He wouldn't think about the potential mess he'd gotten himself into or the hope he'd given Taryn Quinn. He couldn't remember the last time he'd acted impulsively like that. If he didn't feel so good about it, if he couldn't imagine Taryn's smile right now, he'd be disappointed in himself.

Seven

"It's a mistake."

Leaning against the garage pylon, Cole crossed his arms and responded to Brandon's statement. "Duly noted."

And dismissed.

This morning, Cole had dropped in to this double-story bayside home to find his friend lavishing time and attention on his pride and joy—a vintage Harley-Davidson. He would have offered to help but Cole knew from old. Brandon didn't let anyone near his bike. That the showroom-quality cruiser ever made it out onto the street was a miracle. Guess everyone had their passions. Their weaknesses.

Cole's thoughts veered to Taryn Quinn and her exuberant expression the day he'd given the go-ahead for her location survey. He'd be a liar not to admit he was looking forward to spending time alone with her. And who knew? What she had organized might surprise him. If he'd planned to be away from the station longer, he'd have asked Roman Lyons to take the reins. But he'd only be gone from work Friday. Three days in all. And two nights. Brandon's conversation brought him back. He wanted out from Cole's request that he investigate Eloise.

"From what you tell me," Brandon said, polishing a handlebar as if it were a shapely female limb, "the guy responsible for the attempts on your father's life has gone to his maker."

"So it would seem."

"A death certificate's pretty final."

"What if this guy was a patsy?"

"It's possible. Has your father's man mentioned anything about inconsistencies with regard to Eloise's loyalties?"

"Not as yet."

"Like I said." In a white tee and faded jeans, Brandon straightened his linebacker shoulders and snapped the polishing rag at the air. "You want her tailed? Big mistake."

"That's my call." Cole wanted Eloise cleared of all suspicion, if only for his own peace of mind. "Tell me what you know so far."

Since their phone call five days ago, Brandon had dug around Eloise Hunter née Warren's background. Born in Atlanta. Current age, thirty-five. Father a political figure. Mother a close friend of Cole's mom. Busted for soft drugs in high school. No conviction.

Polishing the other handlebar now, Brandon confirmed that Guthrie had met Eloise when she was much younger. They caught up again when he flew out to visit his late wife's remaining relatives some months after her death. The subsequent contact between the two gave "consoling the bereaved" a whole new nauseating meaning.

Cole pushed off the pylon. "Stick with it. And can you look into my father's new housekeeper while you're at it? Nancy Someone-or-other. She's far too creepy to be actually guilty of anything. Still…"

Brandon chuckled. "Not your type?"

Remembering the mustache, Cole shuddered. "Not by any stretch."

Brandon ran a palm over the gleaming crimson fuel tank. "So what *is* happening with your love life?"

"What love life?"

"That's what I figured."

"I'm busy."

"Remember that sweet thing you dated in our Navy Cadet days? Don't think you've had a steady relationship since."

"A year-long crush on a lieutenant's daughter isn't a steady relationship."

"Dear, sweet Meredith McReedy. She broke your heart."

"Like an egg in a skillet," Cole confirmed with a grin, "and she didn't even know it."

"Selfish female, moving interstate and leaving you behind to pine."

"I got over it. Eventually."

"Wonder if she'll be at the reunion tonight." Brandon glanced up from tossing the cloth in his special blue bike-cleaning bucket. "You're going, right?"

"I received the invitation."

"Don't avoid my question."

Heading down the drive toward his car, Cole lowered the sunglasses perched on his crown onto his nose. "I'm beyond all that."

"Beyond catching up with friends?"

"Everyone's married now. I can do without the questions. *When are you settling down? Why haven't you got kids yet?* Last reunion, the woman I took along got it into her head I should fall down on one knee and propose."

Brandon's big hands found his jeans' waistband. "I'm sure you can come up with a few more excuses if you really try."

"You're taking someone?"

Brandon was never without a lady on his arm—a little like Dex, only his brother's affairs were usually plastered across the pages of numerous gossip magazines. Brandon was far more discreet.

"I've asked an interesting lady I met a few weeks ago."

"*Weeks,* did you say?" Cole's lips twitched as he opened the driver's side door. "Must be serious."

"Don't panic. No starry eyes on either side. We have more of a love/hate thing going on."

"Must be going around."

Leaning a forearm along the window edge, Cole spilled all about the delectable, infuriating Taryn Quinn—how he was attracted to her on a number of levels despite the fact that he'd soon need to terminate her contract.

Cole ended, "Then I'll be the one needing a bodyguard."

Brandon's eyebrows hitched. "Fiery, huh?"

"On occasion."

"Sounds interesting. Bring her along."

"She barely tolerates me."

"Oh, *and* she has brains."

Cole grinned. "As a matter of fact, she does."

"What's her story? Why isn't she attached?"

"That's a question I've asked myself."

Brandon's hands dropped to his sides. "You sound suspicious."

"No. Not anymore. Just curious."

The friends said goodbye. A moment later, hand on the ignition, Cole stopped to wonder. Should he invite Taryn to that reunion? Business issues aside, he did find her intriguing. Certainly she'd doused him in wine and had tried to put him in his place more than once. He'd responded by giving in to her—defending her—in ways that, frankly, astounded him.

Worried him.

Grunting, he kicked over the engine and shifted the gears into Reverse.

He didn't need more trouble. No way would he invite her to that reunion tonight. If the idea ever crossed his mind again, he'd make an appointment to have his head examined.

* * *

Taryn peered down at her cell's caller ID and froze.

She'd survived a whole five days at Hunter Broadcasting. Why was Cole calling her on a Saturday? Unless it was to tell her that the location survey scheduled for next weekend was off...that he'd only been teasing and of course he had no plans to consider her show.

She simply wouldn't pick up.

"Is that your phone ringing, sweetheart?" a voice called out from the kitchen.

Sitting on her modest home's back landing step, Taryn answered her aunt, who had dropped in as she did from time to time.

"Don't worry, Vi. I've got it."

She glared at the buzzing cell for a drawn-out moment and Vi's voice came again.

"Is something wrong?"

She didn't know. Didn't want to know. Then again, she'd go crazy waiting until Monday if she didn't find out.

Taryn braced herself. Stabbed the green key.

Cole Hunter's deep voice echoed down the line. "Sorry to disturb you out of work hours."

Taryn quivered at the same time she shrank into herself. She wanted to say, "Get it over with." Instead she said, "That's okay. I'm not doing anything special."

"It's Saturday."

She frowned. Waited. "Uh-huh."

A few seconds passed, long enough for Taryn to study the phone to make sure they were still connected.

"Thing is," Cole finally said, "I wondered if you were doing anything a bit later."

Slanting her head, Taryn cast a glance around the garden. *I'll probably still be sitting here trying to coax a frightened pregnant cat in for shelter before she gives birth.*

"No," she said. "Not especially. Did you want to go over my notes for the survey? I have a ton, although I want to keep the location a secret from you until the end."

She wanted Cole to absorb the undiluted impact when they arrived, which would hopefully inspire as well as challenge him.

When he said, "It's not about the survey," a sick withering feeling dropped through her center. Her mouth went slack. This was it. The "don't come back Monday" call. The end.

"You might remember that I mentioned many years ago I was a Navy Cadet. There's a reunion on tonight. I wondered if you might consider coming along."

She listened harder. There had to be more because this didn't make sense. A reunion? Had she missed something?

"Taryn? You there?"

"I'm not certain I understand."

"I'm inviting you out. Tonight. With me."

He meant on a *date*? Now she was *really* confused.

"If you're busy," he said, "of course I understand."

"I'm not busy."

"So you'll come?"

That voice from the kitchen again. "Any luck out there? Or is she still hiding?"

Her aunt was talking about the pregnant stray. No joy there. But maybe her luck was changing on another front. Taryn knew Cole was attracted to her, but she couldn't get her head around the idea of this suggestion to mix business with pleasure. Still, if he was in need of a date tonight, could she really refuse? She'd been taken aback when Cole had stopped her earlier this week and, in front of witnesses no less, had told her to go ahead and arrange the survey. And that he'd be going, too.

If he was willing to give an inch or two, shouldn't she reciprocate? She'd already vowed to be accommodating, no matter what. The upside was that she could always use the time tonight to bend his ear more about her show.

When she thought about it that way, she'd be mad to decline.

"What time and where?" she asked.

She heard his intake of air. Relief or disbelief?

"It's black tie. I'll collect you at—"

"No, I'll meet you." She'd find her own way there as well as back. She might want to take advantage of this opportunity, but she didn't need to dwell all night on how they would say good-night. A shake of hands in the car? A brush of lips against her cheek at the door?

Awkward.

Cole gave an address and a time. Taryn had ended the call and slumped back against the landing when her aunt appeared with a fresh bowl of cat biscuits. Vi studied her.

"You look like someone just handed you a million dollars."

"Even better. That was my boss."

"Guthrie Hunter. You told me about him. Nice man." Vi set the biscuits down. "*Smart* man."

"No. His son. Cole."

"Calling you on a weekend? Has something come up at the studio?"

Taryn had worked long enough in television for her aunt to know the lingo, the oftentimes crazy hours.

"It wasn't about work. Or not directly. He kind of, well, asked me out. A black-tie event tonight."

"And you said yes?" When Taryn nodded, Vi grinned from ear to ear. "You haven't gone out and enjoyed yourself in such a long time."

"It's not like that. I don't actually *like* him. Cole Hunter is arrogant. Ruthless…"

But her aunt was busy checking the ornate silver wristwatch she'd owned for decades. "If you want to get your hair done, it's already after eleven. Do you have something to wear?"

"A gown I bought for last year's awards ceremonies."

Full length. Sequined. Very Hollywood. Taryn cringed. Hopefully it wouldn't be over-the-top.

She caught her aunt smiling again and pursed her lips.

"Don't get all excited. Tonight isn't like that, okay? Even if I did want to settle down in a relationship—" and she didn't "—Cole's not that type." *Not my type.*

"How do you know?"

"Spend five minutes with the guy."

He had little time for anything other than work and bossing people around. She was amazed he had any personal life.

A noise filtered over from the garden…bushes rustling then a flash of yellow fur. That cat poked its whiskers out between some leaves but, in a heartbeat, vanished again. Taryn thumped a floorboard. She'd been trying to lure that poor cat out for weeks. She looked so mangy Taryn knew she must be without a home. And yet she resisted.

"Maybe she's happier that way," Taryn murmured, thinking aloud. "Maybe she's happier on her own."

Vi patted her niece's shoulder. "Don't give up. Everyone wants companionship. Someone to care for them. Even the most unlikely types."

Eight

He'd told Taryn 7:00 p.m. Black tie. When she'd insisted she find her own way, given the debacle that evening at Marco's when she'd wanted to escape but couldn't, he guessed he understood.

But as seven had wound on to half past, the shine on his understanding had begun to tarnish. At quarter to eight, he was debating whether to call to check up, stride into the party alone or forget about this reunion deal altogether. He had work he could be doing. Going over that football proposal, for one. Instead he was standing here, waiting, waiting. He must look like an overdressed idiot. He knew he felt like one.

Then a silver service cab swerved up. *She* got out. And Cole's chest expanded on a deep breath.

As usual, Taryn Quinn was all grace. Her evening gown—a silver sequined sheath—fit her body like a high-fashion glove. The neckline was a modest scoop, but as she turned to set her stilettos correctly on the pavement, he saw that the back was cut low enough to hover on the edge of X-rated. She spotted him standing alone at the entrance of the inner-city five-star establishment and sent a little wave. He waved back.

Her hair always looked great…a long bouncy blond river.

But tonight, beneath the city lights, it surrounded her face like a luxurious halo. And those lips, my God... Even from a distance, they looked tasty.

Cole met her at the bottom of the steps.

"Nice tux," she said.

"What? This old thing?"

She laughed and something new lifted up inside of him. "You said it was black tie. I took a chance and believed you."

"That's a stunning gown."

"Thank you."

"You look beautiful." Incredible.

Her brow pinched as if she wondered if he were only teasing, before her easy smile shone again. "Sorry I kept you waiting. The cab took forever."

He threaded his arm through hers. "Absolutely no need to apologize."

Inside the ballroom, soft music played while guests churned around, nibbling salmon and caviar canapés while reminiscing. Both he and Taryn accepted chilled flutes from a passing waiter. As she sipped, Cole noticed the flute hovered longer than necessary, covering her smile. Grinning, too, he let his gaze sweep over the glittering room.

"What's funny?"

"It's just since you mentioned the navy, I had visions of scores of officers dressed up in crisp white suits and matching gloves."

"You're partial to a man in uniform?"

Her eyes glistened beneath the lights. "Why? Do you have one hanging at the back of your wardrobe?"

"Hate to admit it but, as a cadet, I looked more like Popeye in my sailor's suit."

Her head went back and her hair bounced around her shoulders as she laughed. "Popeye? Well, at least you're honest. Was there a Brutus in your unit of cadets?"

"Sure. Big, burly, shaving daily by age ten. This guy's better looking than his cartoon counterpart, though."

Her gaze veered to the left. "Would that be him?"

Angling around, he spotted Brandon winding through the crowd. Cole grinned. "Guess the shoulders gave it away."

Brandon stopped before them, tipping his head at Taryn as he introduced himself. "And you must be the mysterious Taryn Quinn."

"Mysterious?" She smiled. "Maybe more your everyday working-class girl."

Brandon's expression said plainly not. And he was right. Taryn was a beauty wearing office garb. But in this glittering silver number, she could put a supermodel out of a job. Her aura was magnetic, her laugh, infectious. He couldn't remember feeling this proud standing beside a date in his life. Those old feelings for Meredith McReedy were left for dead in the shade.

Brandon must have been thinking the same. He was searching the room. When he beckoned someone over, Cole recognized the woman. Barely.

Meredith McReedy bounced straight up, then, on her toes, planted a smacking kiss on Cole's chin. Her lips were so rouged, he just knew she'd left a big red dot.

"Cole, we missed you at the last reunion." Meredith smiled at Taryn, an honest expression, which was nice given the difference in their appearance. While Taryn came off statuesque, poised and glamorous, Cole wasn't certain what had happened to his erstwhile love. Meredith filled them in.

"I'm married now. Three children under four. We're the happiest little family." Meredith spoke directly to Taryn. "You must be Cole's wife."

"Not wife," Cole cut in.

Meredith gave his lapel a playful slap. "You can't hide from responsibility forever."

Cole coughed. Him hiding from responsibility. That was a new one.

With a "We'll catch up later," Meredith disappeared into the tide.

Grinning, Brandon raised his beer. "Well, she looks happy."

Cole narrowed his eyes at his friend. If Brandon was thinking about blabbing, Taryn didn't need to know the background.

"Are you in the forces?" Taryn asked Brandon as the music changed and more couples headed for the dance floor.

"I own a security firm. I do some private investigating from time to time."

"Must be exciting."

"It can be," Brandon said, "when you're on to something with substance."

Her brow wrinkled. "What do you mean?"

"Sometimes a client gets it into his head to chase dead ends."

"No stone left unturned," Cole reasoned, then saw Taryn looking between the two, wondering. He changed the subject. She didn't need to know about Guthrie's recent woes, either.

He asked Brandon, "So, where's your date?"

"You know how I said we have a love/hate relationship? Right now, she's not feeling the love. In fact, I think it's fair to say the curtain has dropped on that particular union."

Taryn's shoulders fell. "I'm sorry to hear that."

Gaze on the filling dance floor, Brandon sipped his beer, swallowed. Exhaled. "Yeah, well, she's missing out. Marissa loves to dance."

"You do, too?" Taryn asked.

"With the right girl," Brandon said.

"You never know." Taryn's smile was encouraging. "Maybe you'll find someone nice to dance with tonight."

Brandon cocked his head then shifted his focus to Cole, arching a brow as if asking permission.

Setting both his and Taryn's flutes on a passing waiter's tray, Cole gave Brandon a "she's mine" look and led Taryn away for a dance of their own.

When they reached the floor, Cole half expected Taryn to kick up a fuss, maybe tell him that coming here was one thing, but dancing cheek to cheek was definitely another. Instead, in her glittering gown, which threw occasional sparks off beneath a slow spinning light, she stood calmly before him. Gaze fixed on his, she waited for his arm to wind around and tug her close.

He was happy to oblige.

Her dress rustled as his hand grazed over her waist then slid down until his palm rested on the bare small of her back. When he pressed enough to let her know she should come closer, she stepped into his space. He took her slim warm hand in his and her head tilted back as she drew in a long breath. Then her hand found his shoulder and, with other couples weaving around, they began to move.

"I like your friend," she said as her fingers on his shoulder scrunched a little then splayed.

"He's one of a kind."

"Good at his work, I assume."

"The best."

"A private investigator."

"That's right."

She looked down then back into his eyes. "Cole, you don't have him investigating me, do you?"

"No." He rotated her around. "I've decided I don't need to rattle your skeletons."

A smile touched her eyes but then she blinked. "He is working for you, though."

He exhaled. "There's been a couple of incidents."

"Concerning you?"

"My father."

Her expression fell and dancing stopped. "Is Guthrie in trouble?"

Peering down into those beautiful concerned eyes, Cole set his jaw. Why the media hadn't got ahold of the story was beyond him, but he didn't expect that to last. Someone somewhere only needed to slip a scrap of information and, next thing, this attempted-murder business would be all over the news. He'd already decided that he wouldn't share any of this with Taryn. Hell, he rarely shared *anything* personal with *anyone*.

But, for whatever reason, he wanted to tonight.

Cole retold the story surrounding the attempts on Guthrie's life, how Jeremy Judge had practically sewn up the case in a twenty-four-hour window and, finally, how he wasn't satisfied this was over.

Taryn shook her head in disbelief. "No wonder you're irritable."

Suppressing a grin, he moved her around in a tight circle. "I'm always irritable."

"I'm serious. I'd be frantic if Vi's life was in danger."

"Vi?"

"My aunt. She brought me up after…"

Her eyes glistened before her gaze skirted away. Obviously too personal. Cole got that.

He was about to say, "You don't have to talk about it," when she found his gaze again and explained.

"I didn't know either of my parents. I was too young to have any memories of that time, but I still wish things had been different. Normal."

The best he could offer was a supportive smile. She'd said so much with so few words. Now *he* couldn't find one.

"I grew up with my aunt," Taryn went on. "Vi's the best there is. She's crazy about cats. She was over today when you phoned. She likes to drop in, you know, but she doesn't smother me like I've heard some parents do." Her brow pinched and he felt her pull back an inch. "I'm boring you."

His gaze brushed her cheek, her lips. "I don't think that's possible."

Beneath the soft lights it was difficult to say, but he thought she might have blushed. Then he felt her draw away a little again. Put that wall back up between them.

"Do you miss the sea?" she asked, looking around at the other grown cadets.

"I'd mentioned there was a time I wanted to serve on a ship. I also thought I might buy a boat-building company and make my own. I imagined doing test runs all day long, standing bold and brave behind the wheel."

He was grinning, mocking himself, but Taryn's face was set.

"Why didn't you?"

He didn't have to think. "Obligation. Duty."

"To your family and Hunter Enterprises."

He nodded.

"So you enjoy what you do there?" she asked.

Searching her eyes, he gave a meaning-filled smile. "Some days are better than others."

"And some days you get lumbered with problems you could do without."

She was talking about her show, but her open look said she wasn't baiting him.

"There are positives to every situation."

"I agree." She seemed to gather herself, gather the words. "I haven't officially thanked you for approving my survey yet."

No, she hadn't. But...

His gaze dropped to her lips again when he said, "It's not too late."

When her head angled, questioning and understanding at

the same time, his pulse kicked, flames raced through his blood and impulse won out. His head lowered over hers.

Beneath his palm, he felt her quiver. Over the music's percussion beat, he heard her sigh. His lips parted slightly as her face tilted more, slanting at the perfect angle to greet him.

Then, as if someone had stuck her with a pin, her eyes rounded and, unraveling herself, she stepped well away.

"I'm not…" She brushed back a tumble of hair fallen over one eye then met his gaze again. "I wasn't expecting that."

"I should apologize." He chanced a smile. "But I'm not sorry."

In fact, truth be told, he wanted to bring her close and finish what he'd started.

Cole felt a tap on his shoulder and, realizing where he was—in a highly public setting—looked back. A man Cole remembered from his cadet days was straightening his bow tie, speaking to him but looking at Taryn.

"I wondered if I could beg a dance from the most beautiful woman in the room."

Without apology, Cole ground out, "Not now," then escorted her off the floor.

Keeping control was hard enough when they were in a room full of people. God help him when they were away on that survey. The way she'd almost surrendered just now, God help them both.

Nine

Throughout the evening, Taryn was introduced to some of Cole's friends from his youth. When they were alone, they talked about work, but neither broached the subject of that dance. Or of that near-miss kiss.

It was as if they'd both silently agreed never to mention it. Forget it had ever happened. Only Taryn doubted she could ever forget that swirling giddy feeling of surrender. The pull at her core was near impossible to resist. If she hadn't experienced the sensation for herself, she simply wouldn't have believed it existed.

But Cole was her *boss*. The future of her beloved project lay in his hands. Her physical side might have longed for his mouth to cover hers…for him to sweep her up and away somewhere ultraprivate. Her rational side, however, warned that clearly she was losing her mind. If they got involved, the lines would be forever blurred. It was bad enough fighting to keep him from tossing her out of Hunters on her ear. How much worse to be sacked and left to rot by someone who had held you? Kissed you?

Humiliating, to say the least.

* * *

The following week at work, although they were pleasant and spoke, neither she nor Cole discussed that evening. When Friday morning rolled around—the day they were scheduled to fly out—Taryn was excited. This was an important step toward seeing her show actually on the air. She was also near paralyzed with dread and fear. What if Cole got too close again? Forget that. Given her reaction when he'd held her on that dance floor, what if at some point she lost all reason and tried to kiss *him*?

By the time she'd finished packing, Taryn had come to a conclusion. One step at a time. If Cole tried to weave his magic over her—if she felt as if she wanted to be seduced—she would cross that burning bridge when she came to it.

At 9:00 a.m., Taryn answered a knock on her door.

Looking mouthwateringly sexy in a pair of dark blue jeans, Cole spotted her luggage waiting in the foyer.

"That's one serious-looking suitcase. We're only away for two days, right?"

Cole had insisted he drive them to the airport. He was here thirty minutes early, but she wasn't ready to leave just yet. She wasn't particularly comfortable with him watching her finish up here, either.

Dragging her gaze away from the V of bare chest visible above the opening of his shirt, she headed off with him following. "I have a few things to tidy up before we leave."

In the kitchen, she pulled a bag of cat biscuits from the pantry while Cole strolled over to her Formica counter.

"You have a cat?"

"She's not mine. Not really."

"Then why are you feeding it?" he asked as she set the food bowl down outside the back door and brought the water bowl in for a refill.

"*It* has a name. Muffin."

"Cats have name tags now?"

"She's a stray. But she's yellow and fluffy like a vanilla cake." Muffin just seemed to fit. She crossed back over to place the fresh water outside, too. "She's close to giving birth."

"Well, do you think you should encourage her?"

She sent him a look. "I can't just leave her and her kittens to starve, or be picked off by birds and snakes. I'd bundle her up and take her to the vet if I could get close enough. Even with her big belly, she's too quick to catch."

"Maybe she's a free spirit." He shrugged. "Maybe she doesn't want a home."

Taryn remembered saying the same thing to Vi last week. But her aunt was right. No one, and that included a cat, chose to be without someplace to feel safe and warm and wanted.

As she turned back from locking the door, Cole's cell phone beeped. He spoke for a couple of minutes then, thoughtful, slotted the phone away.

Moving to the sink, she asked, "Something up at the station?"

"No. That was Brandon checking in."

"More news on your father's situation?"

The sleeves of Cole's casual white button-down were rolled to below the elbow. Now he rested two bronzed forearms horizontal on the counter and absently rotated the platinum watchband circling one wrist, a habit that, she'd noticed, he'd inherited from his dad.

"Seems the man who Jeremy Judge chased in front of that car had a gripe with Hunter Enterprises News division. A year ago he spoke with one of our reporters about a financial institution moving to foreclose on his mortgage. The editor didn't pick up the story. When the man's home went under, he decided to blame us. Brandon hasn't been able to find anything else remotely criminal in his background." He rotated the watchband again. "His wife had left him. Kids are grown-up, moved away."

To Taryn's mind that made the situation all the worse. Sounded like that man had no one to turn to, no one to listen. Maybe he felt he had nothing to live for, which made the "falling under a car" part of the story more believable. All his problems were over now.

At the meals table, she collected a vase then crossed to drop dried blooms and brittle leaves into the trash. She adored choosing flowers for their perfume and color. It was her weekly indulgence. She only wished they lasted longer.

Cole had strolled over to a window. Drawing back the curtain, he scanned the scene outside. Was he looking for the cat, or something—someone—more sinister?

"The gunman didn't have a psychiatric history." He dropped the curtain. "Guess tough times can bring out the worst in us all."

Perhaps, but, "People have choices."

His smile was curious. Maybe admirable. "A woman of integrity."

"What are we without it?"

"Ask my siblings. Wait. I take that back. Wynn at least tries."

Filling the vase with water to soak, Taryn reminded herself, Wynn was the brother who looked after the magazine arm of Hunters in New York.

"He has good intentions," Cole said, checking his cell again. "But I'm afraid my younger brother has a tendency to think with his heart before his brain. Which is probably better than Dex's drawback."

Dex…Cole's movie-making brother in L.A., Taryn thought, checking the setting then clicking on the dishwasher.

"He's got it up here as far as business is concerned." Cole

tapped his temple. "Unfortunately he prefers to think with lower portions of his anatomy."

"I've read about his exploits," she said.

"I doubt he'd mind me saying that was skimming the surface."

"What do your brothers think about their father's situation?"

He followed as she moved around the house, making certain windows were locked.

"We shared a conference call," Cole said. "Wynn and Dex both want to fly out, give him some moral support. See if there's anything they can do."

"Your brothers aren't all bad, then."

She glanced over her shoulder. Cole's expression had turned wistful, as if he might be remembering happier times. Then his brows knitted again.

"I couldn't get in touch with Teagan."

"Your sister." She locked the last window. "She seems to keep a low profile. She's never mentioned in the gossip mags."

"When she was a kid, Teagan was a showstopper. Quick-witted, pretty as a bell, talented. She used to make us all sit down and watch her Spice Girls performances. Being the baby *and* the only girl, she got damn near everything she wanted."

Back in the foyer now, where her luggage waited, Taryn grinned. As if any Hunter child would have done without.

"What does she do in the company?"

"Teagan wants nothing to do with Hunter Enterprises. She calls her lack of interest 'independence.' I call it ingratitude. She runs her own fitness business out of Washington."

"You don't talk?"

"Not for a while."

"So Teagan's the stray who doesn't want a home?"

He did a double take then gifted her one of those sexy grins that secretly made her melt. "Guess she is."

Taryn caught the time on the wall clock. Her stomach jumped. Cole had arrived early, but now they were in danger of running late.

"We'd better go." She extended her bag's handle. "Don't want to miss the flight."

"Which is to where exactly?"

"Let's say a place where the sun and sea rule."

"And *that* narrows it down."

"All I can add is that I hope you packed sunscreen."

A thought exploded in Taryn's mind—a forgotten item—and she rushed into her bedroom with her bag rolling behind. She'd do her work, but she planned to have a window of time off, too. Her already stuffed bag could hold two more teeny-weeny can't-do-without pieces.

Ten

After six hours in the air, and within ten minutes of leaving the much smaller connecting flight, Cole decided that their destination should be named "Taryn Quinn has Rocks in her Head."

For some crazy reason, when Taryn had said she was surveying a location for her *Hot Spots* proposal, Cole had assumed luxury, first-class transportation and air-conditioned comfort at the very least. When she'd let on that they were ultimately destined to land somewhere in Polynesia, his assumptions seemed assured. Now, edging into the decrepit station wagon this island referred to as a taxi, Cole began to grasp the scope of his error.

Luckily the rust bucket was fitted with seat belts.

As the driver roared the gears into a crunching first and slammed his foot to the floor, Cole held on to the arm sling for grim life. He glanced over at Taryn, sitting beside him on the back-passenger seat, and growled. What the hell was she grinning at?

"Cole, you look surprised."

"What's the name of this place again?"

"Ulani. It means happy or gay."

They hit a massive pothole and Cole's head smacked the cab's sagging ceiling, while, bouncing around, Taryn actually laughed. Worse, she looked gorgeous doing it. Her face free of makeup, her hair loose and tousled, she was nothing short of radiant.

During the week, they'd chatted about this trip, and with such composure an outsider would never have guessed what had transpired on that dance floor almost a week ago. He'd thought about that close-proximity incident often since. If she'd leaned in another inch, it would have been on. Instead she'd pulled away at the last minute and he'd been given space to cool down, keep his head.

Only problem was that stir and urge hadn't left him. He might have behaved civilly this week, but underneath he'd wanted to lay this on the line and take what he believed she wanted to give. He should be dreading these next couple of days. But he was only glad this time had finally come. At last they were alone and this thing simmering between them could come to a head.

But he'd envisaged that would happen amid first-rate treatment and perhaps even satin sheets. Guess he'd get past this shock.

"Why did you choose this place?"

"I wanted different, out of the ordinary," Taryn said, gazing out over a landscape of vine-strangled palms backdropped by a sleeping monster of a volcano. "Anyone can go to Hawaii or Tonga."

"I take it the resort or hotel or wherever you're taking me isn't five-star."

"From the pictures and reviews, I'd give it six."

Another pothole sent him jolting and cringing in his seat again. "I'm thinking a remedial massage is a priority."

"I could always organize the next flight out for you," she offered.

"And miss all the fun?"

The taxi skidded to a stop. Cole shifted to inspect the building and his jaw dropped. This place wasn't much better than a shack.

He drawled, "You are kidding."

"Not even a little bit."

"Didn't you say that night at Marco's, and I quote, 'This program could start a whole new genre'?" He examined the gray-bearded dog asleep on its back in a most unflattering pose near the entrance. "Maybe we *should* head back," he muttered under his breath.

Did she really have no idea? More than ever before, after seeing this, chances were her show was dead in the water. Only a miracle could save it now.

The driver was lugging both her suitcase and his overnighter toward that reception shack. Above a barely hinged door rested a lopsided sign, which read in faded green paint, WEL OME.

"There's still time to escape," she told him slipping out of the taxi, whereupon Cole set his teeth, ran a hand through his hair then scraped himself out of the vehicle, too.

"I'll stay," he said, dragging his feet to follow, "if only to see what you think can possibly keep an audience glued to their seats."

As well as the promise of being alone with you.

In her tantalizing fitted blue wrap dress, she continued on with a laugh. Seeing those long tanned legs in that dress, that heavenly behind swaying as if to beckon him near…

Cole's pace picked up.

Sure. He could slum it for a couple of days.

From the moment they touched down, Taryn had fallen in love with this tropical oasis. As far as she was concerned, a weekend wasn't nearly long enough. Except, of course, she'd need to contend with the "Cole looking extra hot in casual wear" situation. But truth was she'd find him sexy even in his Popeye suit.

At a bamboo reception counter, a friendly middle-aged lady with oversize dentures and a gold-plated name tag that read Sonika checked their reservation, after which a man, naked from the waist up, collected their bags. Standing beside her, Taryn sensed Cole's masculine sensitivities prickle. Perhaps he was anticipating an equally stunning island girl to materialize and show off *her* assets. Best he didn't hold his breath. This island was particularly "woman user friendly."

Sonika's smile beamed brighter. "I'm sure you will be happy with your accommodation," she said in accented English. "Your bungalow has one of the best views on the island."

"How many guest bungalows do you have here?" Cole asked.

"Only six on the whole island. The other five are occupied," she said, closing her registry book. "But don't worry that you'll run into anyone if you don't want to. Privacy is our promise."

The man and his WrestleMania shoulders ushered them out a side door and down a long sandy path, which was bordered by lush ferns and palm trees on either side. Above them curious monkeys crouched on branches, a menagerie of birdlife hooted and cooed, heady combinations of floral scents filled the air and Taryn wanted to sigh. These surroundings would make for fabulous visuals and audio. All she needed was that final nod. She hoped Cole would be a good sport and admit this ultraexotic location and her idea were winners…that is, when he got over the next surprise.

A few minutes later, they arrived at their bungalow. While the porter continued on to drop their bags inside, a previously tetchy Cole seemed to enjoy a change of heart.

"I must say, I had my doubts." He scooped up a handful of powdery sand and let it filter through his fingers while surveying a bay that spread out before them like an endless throw of mirror-blue silk. "Not the Hilton but that *is* an exceptional view." He spotted a calico hammock waiting on the bungalow's porch and rubbed his shoulder. "I can picture myself swaying in that. In fact…"

But as he moved toward the steps and that hammock, Taryn crossed to block his path.

"I'm afraid you have a task or two to perform before you can lie back," she said.

"We'll take an hour to rest up before we start on your survey work."

"I'm not talking about that. When a person comes to this Polynesian island, there are certain…requirements. Duties."

"What do we have to do?"

"Not we. *You.*"

He threw another glance around and coughed out a laugh. "Like hunt down a wild boar? Descend into the fiery bowels of a live volcano?" When her expression held, his smirk died. "Please tell me that volcano isn't live."

"Remember I said that this island's name means *happy.* This place is also meant to be a sanctuary where individuals come to know and appreciate others and, more importantly, understand themselves."

He waited then finally shrugged. "And…?"

"Women here, Cole, are adored and revered. They're waited on hand and foot."

Trying to absorb the concept, he repeated her words. "Women are waited on here…"

"Yes. Hand and foot."

"So where's your slave?"

"Standing right there."

Cole actually looked over his shoulder. When he realized the joke was on him, he slowly turned back. She'd had fun imagining this moment. He'd invited himself along to see for himself. Like the emperor with his new clothes, Cole had gotten his wish. If he had half a funny bone, he'd take it on the chin. Hell, he might even laugh. But his expression fell flat.

"Other than the view and that hammock," he said, "you're not scoring too many points."

A bristle ran up the back of her neck. At times he could be so darn negative. "You don't have to stay if you can't handle it."

He challenged her gaze for a long moment then bent to slip off his loafers and wiggled his toes in the sand.

"But if I leave you here all alone," he said, "who will brush your hair? Peel your grapes?"

At that moment, that man with his amazing tan and billboard chest passed by. When he sent a dazzling helpful smile her way before leaving by the path again, Taryn sucked down a breath and gathered her thoughts.

Cole wanted to know who would peel her grapes?

Winding her arms over her waist, she angled her head and shrugged. "Oh, I'm sure I'll find someone."

From the way Cole's shoulders squared, he was back to unimpressed mode. "I thought you were selling this as a family show."

"I'm sure a lot of underappreciated mothers would love a slot."

"What's in it for the poor lugs who have to tag along?"

"Quality time to reflect?"

"While they're fanning the revered ones with palm fronds, I suppose."

"And all while enjoying that view." When his unimpressed look held, she spelled it out. "This island's magic lies in its reversal of social domestic norms. It encourages men to truly nurture their women, which will hopefully ultimately deepen and strengthen their relationships. You've heard of the saying, with sacrifice comes great reward? In the work comes the reward. The payoff."

"With sacrifice comes reward."

She nodded then headed toward the bungalow. "But, before you get busy peeling any fruit, we should unpack."

Cole massaged his brow. He was *her* boss. So why was he being bossed around? Oh, that's right. This "women are revered, men are slaves" twist. Novel. Cute.

Taryn was strong-willed. Even on her best behavior, she couldn't help but occasionally mock him. Over this past week, he'd almost gotten used to her particular brand of sass. She had a sharp wit. Sometimes *too* sharp. And he didn't enjoy being anyone's pincushion.

She'd told him that he needed to unpack.

He called out, "We're here two days."

"Clothes get rumpled."

"We're not dining with the queen."

On the bottom step, she rotated around. "If you want to live out of a bag, that's your business."

Darn right it was his business. This might be her location survey but, make no mistake, he was in charge regardless of this island's female bias. And as she continued up those steps in that hug-every-curve dress, a cog in his brain turned and clicked. When she reached the bungalow doorway, the ideal solution to this predicament lit his mind like the breaking of tomorrow's dawn.

Taryn wanted to explore the island's ethos. She expected him to serve. Get enlightened.

He called out again. "I might not need to unpack my bag but, if I have this setup right, while we're here—me being the male and you being the female—I'm supposed to revere you. Be your slave."

Pivoting again, she rested a hand on the bamboo doorjamb. "*Slave* was your term."

"But *Hot Spots* male guests here will be expected to look after any chores so their wife or girlfriend can lie back and soak up the atmosphere. That's the twist—the opportunity for confrontation and redemption—you want the contestants and viewers to experience, right?"

"Right."

"Which means, if we're really going to get a take on possible dynamics, while I might not want to unpack my bag, I should 'servant up' and unpack yours."

As he sauntered up the steps, she arched a brow. "We don't need to go to extremes."

"Do you want me to immerse myself in this project or don't you? Heaven forbid a rumor should spread that I didn't play by the rules and robbed you of a fair chance."

"I'm quite capable—"

"Then again if you don't want to give it your best shot…"

She seemed to hold her breath. As he imagined her heart pounding and thoughts racing, Cole contained his grin. She was embarrassed and uncertain and probably nudging toward really annoyed at this point. But she'd set the agenda and, as far as he could see, she'd left herself no room to back out.

"Just leave what's in the zipped pouch," she finally said.

"Sure. You go mix yourself a piña colada and leave all the work to me." He set a fingertip to his cheek. "Although shaking cocktails must be my job, too. Maybe wiggle your toes in the sand until I can be of further service."

Passing on his way inside the bungalow, Cole rolled a hand—a theatrical motion from forehead to waist—while, feeling robbed, Taryn moved down the steps and into the clearing.

Above her, palms fronds swayed and clacked in a gentle sea breeze. Like a balm, the sun's heat soaked into her skin. The salty scent drifting in from the Pacific was nothing short of drugging. Paradise. She'd promised herself, no matter what, she would find a little time to unwind.

But she'd been kidding herself. While Cole was around that would never happen. Yes, she'd planned to put him on the spot with that "women are revered" policy. She'd wanted him to squirm but more so think about setup in relation to ratings ramifications for her show. Not for one minute did she buy his spiel about being happy to serve. She had the biggest feeling he was up to something. Something that might leave her squirming instead of him.

A rustling in the brush drew her attention. From a mass of ferns, a boy aged six or seven appeared. He had the biggest, brownest eyes Taryn had ever seen. Wearing that blue-striped tee and toothy grin, he was positively disarming. Striding right up, he gestured toward her feet then indicated she should sit in a deck chair positioned to one side of the bungalow steps.

Wanting to ruffle his mop of clean dark hair, she laughed. "Thank you, but I'm not tired." She crouched to speak face-to-face. "What's your name?"

But the boy was already scurrying off back into the ferns. The next second, Cole's voice boomed out from the bungalow.

"Where do you want me to put these?"

She swung around. Cole stood in the doorway. He held her bikini top in one hand, her bottoms in the other.

After the blush had whooshed up from her toes to her crown, she got her mouth to work and very calmly asked, "What do you think you're doing?"

"Unpacking, as per instructions."

"I told you to stay away from the zip."

"These were right on top."

As he jiggled the top then the bottoms in turn, her thoughts rewound. Usually she put her delicates in a zipped compartment to keep them separate and easy to access. But when she'd remembered her bathing suit this morning at the last minute, she'd shoved it inside her case on top of everything else.

And, honestly—so what? They were two pieces of Lycra. Women had worn them for decades. And yet the way he was holding them, the ties twined loosely around those strong tanned fingers, she felt so suddenly flustered, as if he'd removed them not from her luggage but fresh off her body. His next comments made it all ten times worse.

"Interesting work attire, Miss Quinn." He pushed a sigh out over the hint of a grin. "And I thought you were serious about this weekend."

That flustered feeling stirring her insides swelled into something far more dangerous. She'd known he was hatching something he'd find amusing. Something to put her in her place. She strode up the steps and snatched both pieces from his grasp. Incredibly, he didn't laugh, didn't even smile. Rather he glanced away and rubbed the back of his neck, as if he felt uncomfortable, which, under the circumstances, she found difficult to believe.

She narrowed her eyes at him. "What's that look?"

"I thought I'd better mention now…"

"Mention what?"

"There's only one bed?"

After a moment of numb shock, she hacked out a laugh. *Ridiculous.* "Of course there's more than *one bed*."

When she'd received her reservation details, she'd been assured of two bedrooms. And on opposite sides of the hut.

"Maybe you should have booked separate bungalows," he said, "just to be sure."

"You heard the woman at the desk. There are only five other bungalows and they're all taken."

Her words trailed as reality tunneled in and set like reinforced concrete. There'd been a terrible mix-up, and even if she had any hope another guest might consider swapping for a single-bedroom bungalow, she wouldn't put Sonika to the embarrassment and trouble. A weekend's accommodation here cost an arm and a leg and they were staying for free. There must be another way. She might find Cole attractive. She might have wondered how these two days would pan out. But she didn't want him to think she'd actually planned it this way.

After running the problem around in her head a few more times, she offered a weak smile. "You did say you liked the hammock."

"You want me to be sucked dry and eaten by mosquitoes?"

"There must be a couch?"

"It's been a while since I slept on a sofa."

"Then *I'll* take the couch."

"If you don't mind the lack of privacy, I won't complain."

Taryn's temper began to boil. Hopefully, she would come away from these two days with that contract for *Hot Spots* finally secured. There was also a chance that before this time was through, she'd regress, give in to temptation and show Cole Hunter again just how much he irritated her.

Right now, he irritated her a lot.

Cole's expression changed; he stiffened then he peered off into the brush. She followed his line of vision. Among the ferns, blue stripes of a tee flashed before all was quiet again.

She explained, "It's a boy. He was here earlier, wanting me to sit down and rest."

"I thought I was in charge of your pampering."

She headed inside to inspect the bedroom situation. "Maybe you've been assigned a helper."

"You think I need help?"

She rolled her eyes. *Let me count the ways.*

In the casual main room, she turned. Cole was standing right behind her. As his gaze intensified and stroked her lips, her breathing came a little quicker and her chin reflexively raised a notch. When his head slanted and deliberately low-

ered closer to hers, for one horrifying moment, she thought
that force urging her to lean in would win.

And maybe she shouldn't fight it. Maybe she should let her
defenses down, throw up her hands and finally give in. Because truth was she wanted to kiss Cole Hunter harder than
she'd kissed any man.

His hands found hers and their fingers tangled together
among those bikini strings. Her eyes drifted shut and, in a
heartbeat, that tingling burn grew into a storm where a thousand shooting flames combined to ignite and consume every
inch of her soul. Suddenly, she felt so dizzy she couldn't think
straight, unless it was to wonder if his mouth was even half
as confident and skilled as instinct said it must be.

Her heavy eyelids dragged opened.

His gaze still on her lips, he lifted her clasped hands to his
hard chest and after a few mind-numbing moments, he smiled
slowly and said, "Know what I'm thinking?"

Her chest rose on a deep breath. "Tell me."

"I'm thinking one bedroom's probably enough."

Eleven

As all the world funneled back and left just the two of them, Cole wondered how he might handle the situation should Taryn suffer a sudden change of heart and, at this last possible moment, step away like she had that night on the dance floor.

But when his arms wove around and gathered her close, she didn't struggle, didn't regroup or seem to rethink. Rather, when he finally claimed that long-anticipated scorching kiss, she melted like warm butter, her lips parting on a sigh that both fed his growing hunger and invited him in. He knew as well as she did—this kiss had always been in the cards. This embrace was only their first.

At the same time as he moved to cradle her nape and slant back her head, his other hand scooped lower…over the slope of her hip then around the tight high curve of her behind. She responded by quivering while her palms cupped his jaw then ironed higher up through his hair. She arched in until they were glued together, front to front.

When their kiss shifted, deepened, nearly every drop of blood he owned flooded and filled his loins. The physical longing gripping every one of his senses was unprecedented. Off the chart. But he needed more. He had to get rid of her dress, his clothes, splay her out on that bed and push up inside of her until she lost her breath and sobbed out his name.

His touch wandered farther, sliding up under the back of her skirt, beneath her panties then down over that sumptuous curve and between her thighs. When he found her so warm and well on the road to ready, his burgeoning erection jerked, demanding to be freed. Scooping her that much closer, his chest rumbled as he thought of the pleasure that lay ahead. As she arched and began to move around his touch, he slid farther in between her thighs until he discovered that tiny ultrasensitive treasure at her rainbow's end.

With a soft groan, she wound her lips away from his, even as her body nudged down against him. He grazed his lips over hers. "The bed's just over there."

Her eyes closed, her brow pinched a little and then she reached behind and gripped his wrist.

"I'm sorry, Cole. We can't do this."

"Of course we can. This has been brewing since the day we met."

"We've known each other two weeks."

He nipped her lower lip. "Now we'll know each other better."

Her eyes dragged open. "Cole, this is a bad idea."

"Does this feel bad to you?"

He claimed her mouth again, and again she dissolved, this time to the point where her knees must have turned to jelly. When she sagged against him, he shifted to sweep her up into his arms. As she pulled herself higher and her breasts ground against his chest, he didn't lighten the kiss. Rather, relying on instinct, he navigated his way toward that bedroom door. But as he made it through, she stiffened and dragged her mouth from his again. Her eyes were glistening, pleading.

"Cole, will we regret this?"

"Trust me." He smiled gently. "We won't."

"You don't want to feel as if you gave me the okay on my show simply because we slept together."

"Don't worry." He lifted her in his arms and nuzzled her sweet-scented neck. "I wouldn't do that."

"You wouldn't?"

She smelled like flowers mixed with sunshine. Her skin was so smooth, he couldn't imagine she'd ever owned a blemish. She murmured his name and Cole remembered her question. Would this sway his decision regarding her show? If anything he was impartial.

He nuzzled more.

Or tried his best to be.

"Business is business," he murmured against her cheek.

"So you could kiss me, make love to me, then change back to being the boss? Being *you?*"

He shifted to look into her eyes. "What's so wrong with being me?"

"Nothing. Usually." She shrugged. "I suppose."

His head went back. "You sure know how to destroy a beautiful moment."

"I was about to say the same."

While his chest tightened, her eyes darkened and the focus of their intensity shifted then changed course. They peered into each other's eyes. Taryn's vision seemed to have gotten clearer.

"I think you should put me down," she said then proceeded to wiggle like a cat getting free from a bag.

His brain said to set her down. This union wasn't happening, or not happening now. But his arms were having a hard time understanding.

She stopped struggling and a shudder of something like panic filtered over her face. "Cole? Please…"

He set her down on both feet and she straightened her dress then her hair.

"I don't think we should do that again," she said.

"You're the one pushing up against me. I was only following orders."

"Don't use that excuse."

"I didn't pack a miniscule bikini."

"And that gives you the right to pounce on me?"

"Look, I put you down. But don't try to tell me that you didn't want that to happen."

"You didn't give me a choice."

"I think you're confused."

"Maybe I am. I know I need some time alone. Some space." Her cheeks flushed, and she nodded at the doorway.

"You want me to leave?"

"In the next five seconds would be good."

Cole dragged a hand down his face. She might not have meant for the situation to get out of hand so quickly, but he'd seen what she'd packed by way of a nightdress and, in his books, baby-doll white lace didn't say "not interested." If she wanted him to go now, he'd go.

But he'd be damned if he'd apologize.

And double damned if this was over.

Hearing Cole thump away across the wood floor, out onto the verandah and hopefully farther into the deep dark never-to-be-seen-again jungle, Taryn bit her lip. What rankled most was the fact he was right. She *had* wanted that kiss. She'd wanted his strong, steady arms around her. At one crazy point, she'd even wanted to fall into bed with him then and there. She examined the rattan ceiling fan, colorful shaggy rug, spray of side-table flowers and a frangipani-print quilt with a mountain of matching pillows. If she'd gone ahead, she and Cole would be on that bed right now, prying off clothes, rejoicing in the hot slick slide of each other's skin....

Taryn hauled herself back.

No matter how strong the attraction, obviously a coming

together with Cole in a sexual sense would be way too complicated. Too much was at stake. Her show. Her job. Her self-respect, as well as other emotions.

But she couldn't change what had happened. She could, however, carry on with her plans for this survey. Cole had admitted that he wouldn't automatically approve her proposal if they'd made love. Which on the flip side meant he shouldn't hold yet another heated episode against her, either. Hell, she'd tossed a glass of wine at him and he hadn't thrown her out.

But there was a part of her that wanted to let Cole know she hadn't forgiven him for teasing her, handling her bikini the way he had. He'd looked so amused by her reaction.

She tugged the tie at the side of her wrap dress.

Well, maybe it was her turn to be amused.

Needing to cool off fast, Cole took a long swim in his Calvin Kleins. When he finally wandered out from the bay, shaking water from his hair, he wished he'd thought to bring a towel. But rather than go inside and meet up with that woman whose mission was to drive him crazy, he'd lie out here on the warm sand. Hopefully, the way his luck was going, a coconut wouldn't fall and crack open his head.

He'd dropped to his knees and was leveling out a piece of sand with a palm while admiring a flock of lorikeets squawking across the flawless blue sky, when Taryn sauntered out from the bungalow and down those steps. As his focus zeroed in, the ground slanted, his heart jumped and Cole had to lean against a nearby boulder to keep from tipping over.

He would have growled. In fact, he did. But the sound he made didn't come from a place of residual annoyance. The vibration rumbling around in his chest, leaking from his throat, was a reaction to the clothes Taryn was wearing. Make that *wasn't* wearing. He couldn't believe she'd actually gone and slipped into that bikini.

He'd imagined the next time they met, Taryn would have resumed her cool. He was right about that. Standing at the bottom of the steps, face tilted upward and enjoying the sunshine, she was as relaxed as they come. She hadn't even draped one of those poolside skirts around her hips in a token show of modesty. If she'd meant to disarm him—show him that this was, in fact, her gig and she'd do as she pleased—well, it had worked.

Glancing around, she caught sight of him. She didn't wave but she did smile, a lazy grin that relayed remarkable confidence. Then she walked straight up to him, heavenly hips swaying as her feet dug in and out of the soft sand. When her knees were at eye level, she stopped. What option did he have but to take a deep breath and look up?

In the direct light, her skin glowed with a natural cinnamon tone. Her legs looked smoother and longer than he'd even imagined. Manicured fingers sat splayed on two mouthwatering hips. She looked down at him as if he were a lost dog she might want to pat, if he behaved.

"How's the water?" she asked, looking out over the bay while her toe absently cut a line in the sand under his nose.

Cole toppled forward but recovered quickly, angling up to sit with one leg bent and a crooked arm resting on that knee. Getting his head back together, he purposely ran an interested eye over her attire.

"You look as if you're about to find out for yourself."

She glanced down as if only noticing she was pretty much naked. "Oh, I slipped these on under some dungarees. I wanted to be comfortable doing an initial scout of the surrounds. I've marked a couple of great spots I'd like to utilize." She reached to lift the hair off the back of her neck. "I'm glad to be out of those work clothes. I've really worked up a sweat."

He stopped staring and clapped shut his mouth. His throat felt thick, his body hard. "You deserve a break."

"I was thinking the same."

He thought a moment, wondering if he should play this aloof like her, but, frankly, he was suffering a twinge of guilt. Why not get it out in the open? Be a man.

"If you wanted to make a point," he said, "consider it made."

"What point would that be?"

"That this is your survey, your time to manage, and maybe I shouldn't have tried to embarrass you earlier by showing off what was obviously private." That being the bikini she didn't seem the least embarrassed about now.

She blinked twice, as if she were surprised by his honesty, then her unaffected air returned. "Is that an apology?"

"With a caveat. By setting me up with this island's 'men are servants' slant, you asked for it."

"The way you provoked me, you deserved it."

He looked heavenward. Blew out a breath. "Fine. Just show a little mercy and go cover up."

Victory sparkled in her eyes, but she kept up the pain and suffering by walking past him to provide an incredible rear view. "It's not as if you haven't seen a woman in a bathing suit before."

"Right now, I can't remember a one."

When she angled around, a frown knotted her brow. Surprise again? Hell, in that swimsuit, she was stunning and she knew it. In fact, Taryn was stunning no matter what she wore. No matter what she did or said or thought.

Out of the corner of his eye, Cole spotted movement: that blue-striped tee he'd seen earlier. The boy Taryn had told him about.

When Taryn spotted the boy, too, her thoughtful look evaporated on a quick smile.

"Hey, you're back," she was saying, but, as quick as a rabbit, the boy already had her hand and was urging her back toward the bungalow. Cole pushed to his feet and, dry enough, stepped into the jeans he'd cast off earlier.

He called after them, "What's the problem?"

The boy didn't acknowledge the question. Rather he kept leading Taryn to the deck chairs.

"He wants me to sit and relax," she said.

Before one of the chairs, the boy set down a tray he'd been carrying. Then he shot off around the corner of the bungalow. In a heartbeat, he'd returned with an old wooden bucket.

Cole moved forward. "What's he up to?"

Taryn was looking at the boy as if he were the most adorable entity on the planet. "I think he's preparing me a footbath."

Cole mentally took a long step back. Wonderful. But he wouldn't get involved in that particular discussion again. If the males here wanted to wait on their women, that was better than great. Junior could slave over footbaths all he pleased. But from now on Cole Hunter was nothing more than a bystander. It was past time he found a cool drink and chilled out in that hammock.

But the boy had skipped up to *him* now and, having grabbed his hand, was pointing at the foliage. Cole gently wound his arm free.

"Sorry, kid. I'm off duty."

Taryn opened her mouth then, sitting down in the chair, shut it tight. As she glared at him, Cole pinned her with a look of his own.

"What?"

"It's just I can't understand how you can ignore that face. Those big brown eyes." Sitting back, she rapped fingertips on the chair arms. "Guess big TV executives don't have time for children."

"As a matter of fact I have a kid brother about his age. Stepmom, remember?"

"Oh." She recovered. "See him much?"

"As much as circumstances allow."

"That often, huh?"

Cole set his jaw. He wouldn't bother to explain.

But now that he looked closer, this boy did share similarities with Tate. Same innocence shining like Christmas lights in his eyes. Same eager look, wanting to hang out.

Cole let the air out of his lungs then surrendered.

"Okay. Where do you want to take me?"

The boy presented his bucket.

"You want this filled?" Cole examined the area, saw an outside faucet and moved to collect the bucket. But the boy shook his head and stabbed a finger toward a track that disappeared in the tropical wild.

Taryn crossed those luxurious long legs. "He wants you to go with him."

When the boy flashed that smile again, Cole scratched his head and muttered, "It's a good thing you're cute." He took the bucket and told Taryn as they headed off, "Try not to miss me."

"How will I cope?"

Cole walked away, a grin tugging one corner of his mouth. Probably best that he remove himself from the scene in any case. Taryn was obviously intent on showing him that she wasn't the least bit fazed by his dangling of that bikini or by that explosive kiss. He wondered if she'd heard the saying: trying a little too hard.

Ten minutes later, he and Junior were weaving through layers of ferns and other undergrowth, which rested beneath a dense canopy of vegetation. As birds whistled and insects clicked, Cole got to wondering how this boy and Tate might get along. Tate could show him how to use his most recent gadget—the one Cole had reset the other night—and this little guy could demonstrate how to catch fish in a handmade net or canoe. Hell, *he'd* even like to try that. Maybe one day he could come back and bring Tate along. He hadn't liked Taryn's remark, but they really didn't spend enough time together.

Eventually they stopped at a freshwater spring surrounded by mossy boulders. Watching a line of small snails slither over a leaf the size of a pizza, Cole hunkered down. It was muggy under the canopy and he'd worked up a sweat. First he splashed water over his head. Then, enjoying the icy trickles trailing down his back, he scooped up a handful and drank. He groaned aloud. It tasted so good and clean. Cole drank his fill then dragged the bucket through the pool.

Heaving the bucket out, he spotted a large red flower fallen to the ground...some kind of hibiscus hybrid. Only the petals were closed up tight, like it was asleep in the middle of the day. Noticing his interest, the boy carefully gathered the flower up. Perhaps he meant to make a gift of it to Taryn. Cole smiled. Nice kid. Obviously brought up the right way.

When the boy looked at him again, Cole asked, "Where are your mother and father?"

Immediately the boy set off along that path again but veered down a different track that was crisscrossed with pygmy palm fronds and littered with color-filled butterflies. After several minutes' journey, a clearing came into view. Pulling up, the boy nodded toward a clutch of bungalows. A score of people in casual Western dress were making meals, crafting woods. Kids laughed as they chased each other around buildings and other structures. When a woman carrying a baby in a sling strolled into view, the boy pointed.

"Your mother?" Cole asked.

The boy spoke a word in his language and nodded. Then, thoughtful, he lowered his gaze to the bloom.

Cole remembered giving garden flowers to his mother when he was around that age. He recalled her loving smiles and warm hugs those times she'd held him close and said, "You're a special boy, Cole."

Nowadays, when he was dating a woman and a birthday or some other occasion came around, he'd choose a nice pendant or bracelet. Might be more the norm, but, to his mind, the giving of flowers in new relationships was too personal. And his relationships rarely lasted past "new." What female would choose a floral arrangement over gold or gems, anyway?

The boy was heading off again with that sleeping flower still protected in the cup of his hands. Cole shifted the bucket to his other hand and followed.

Back at the bungalow, Taryn had indeed shown mercy. A light dress now covering that bikini, she was taking shots of the bay where a pod of dolphins played. Closing his eyes, Cole lifted his nose to the air. God, he loved the smell of the ocean. Taryn had once asked and it was true. If he hadn't been bequeathed a career in television, he'd have found a vocation that took him offshore. He'd sometimes wondered if some sailor or pirate ancestor had passed down the seawater that seemed to flow through his veins.

Her shoulders glowing from their time in the sun, Taryn angled around. "You're back."

"And bearing gifts." Cole presented his bucket.

Lowering her camera, Taryn watched Cole move forward with his bucket and pint-size companion.

"This water is guaranteed to leave your soles feeling like silk," he said as she snapped the cap over her camera lens.

"That good, huh?"

"Just ask the man." Cole glanced down but the boy was already disappearing back into the trees. Grinning, he shrugged. "Busy man."

He moved toward the chairs, obviously preparing to fill that tray.

Taryn wanted to tell him, don't bother. She wasn't taking a footbath. The game of "on this island, men must serve" was over, at least between the two of them. But, caught up in admiring that vision of masculine perfection—all those rippling muscles in Cole's arms and chest as he'd moved toward her—Taryn's thoughts got waylaid. She had appreciated the physique of the man who'd brought down their luggage but, to her mind, Cole's proportions were far more appealing.

His shoulders, she already knew, were delectably broad. The muscles that sloped from the sides of his neck to each shoulder were stacked and those pecs were pure power. Dark crisp hair covered his chest, disappearing where the definition of his abs began and starting again where a trail snaked from below his navel. As he moved past with that bucket, she imagined sliding a hand from his taut belly all the way up to the beating hollow of his throat and quietly sighed.

She had indeed meant to tease him with her bikini show earlier. She'd wanted to leave him gobsmacked and sorry that he'd ever thought to provoke her. But where her state of half undress had been calculated, Cole's current condition was not. He was perfectly comfortable in his body, even if the sight was making *her* mouth water.

Finished filling the tray, he straightened and faced her, gifting her a glorious square-on chest view. Wetting suddenly dry lips, she shrugged and made light.

"You didn't have to do that."

He was running a hand back through hair flopped over his brow. She couldn't resist drinking in the way that biceps hardened and bulged before his arm lowered again.

"Couldn't disappoint our friend, now, could I?" He headed for the steps. "I'm off to check out the drink situation."

"Liqueurs are in the cabinet," she said. "Mixers and wine in the fridge." But she'd spoken before she'd thought. After their passionate embrace earlier, she probably shouldn't be offering alcohol.

But he only said, "A beer'll hit the spot. Can I get you anything?"

When he stopped at the top of the landing and glanced back, looking like a bronzed god from on high, her insides tightened and that pleasant tingling burn began to filter through her veins again. Feeling light-headed, she waved him on.

"I'll grab something with dinner."

Before she'd finished her sentence, his focus shifted and he nudged his chin toward the clearing. "Which, if I'm not mistaken, seems to have arrived."

Three men and two women appeared, carrying in with them enough supplies to feed a king and his court. Good news because Cole was famished. He never found lunch on aircraft particularly satisfying.

While the guys set up a table close to the shoreline, the ladies covered a separate serving table with chowder, shellfish and juicy fingers of papaya. Around thatched food containers sat cracked coconuts filled with salads, tomato flowerets and frangipani leis.

He sauntered down to where Taryn stood watching, too, as their ultraprivate and—dare he say—romantic dinner was arranged.

The sun had begun to slip behind the island's western dome. Shadows cast by the surrounding palm trees had grown a little darker and longer. As a lone petrel flew low over the water, the tip of its wing slicing the glassy surface, the men wedged torches into the sand and, a moment later, mellow flames licked at the coming dusk. After a glass carafe filled with a pale pink drink was set at the center of the meals table, with customary wide smiles, the wait team bowed off.

Stomach growling, Cole rubbed a hand over his chest. "Well, this is special."

"I was emailed images and menus but, yeah…" Taryn moved forward. "This is pretty amazing."

Alone again, Cole retracted the chair placed on her side of the table and Taryn took her seat.

"This kind of scene will make for amazing footage," she said, sweeping a gaze over the tables, the bay and a sapphire sky pinpricked with the earliest awakening of stars.

"I wonder if the natives eat like this every night." Cole pulled in his chair, too. "On our way back from that spring today, our little friend showed me his village. Not a cell phone or laptop anywhere to be seen."

"It's good to turn off the outside world." She flicked out her napkin. "When was your last vacation?"

"I don't have time for vacations."

"You never take time off?"

"Not since my father semiretired." He filled her glass from the carafe then took care of his own. "Can't let the ship go under, remember?"

"You can delegate. Roman could take care of some things."

Cole conceded. "He's come on board, for as long as a week at a time when I've needed him to."

"Then why not take a break? Refill your well?"

"I'm here now, aren't I?" He raised his glass. *Cheers.*

"This isn't supposed to be a vacation." She sipped and sighed at the cool fruity blend he'd already tasted and fallen in love with. "Besides—" she set down her glass "—it's only a couple of days."

"Which I'm rather enjoying." Despite their spat earlier.

"Only goes to show. You should do it more often."

"Guess we should."

Midway through setting down his glass, Cole hesitated. He hadn't meant to respond to her suggestion in the plural. But Taryn didn't bat an eye at his *we* rather than *I*. Instead she reached for a coconut to spoon salad onto her plate, and Cole eased out the breath he'd held.

He didn't intimidate her. Or not for long. In fact, he'd never felt so challenged yet strangely at ease in a woman's company before. She made every other person he'd dated seem staid.

Not that this was a date, Cole reminded himself, spooning salad out for himself...even if, with Taryn's eyes sparkling in the torchlight, nature's music playing a lazy tune, an open-ended evening ahead of them and a bold afternoon behind, it sure was beginning to feel like one.

Twelve

When they'd finished the last of that tasty pink nectar, out of nowhere one of the women who'd set up earlier appeared with a fresh batch. Taryn thought she'd make an inquiry.

"Can you tell me the best direction for a walk along the beach tonight?" She explained to Cole, "I want to take some night shots."

"A full moon will be out," the woman said, refilling their glasses. "Either stretch is free from outcrops. There are more turtle nests down that way." She slanted her head toward their right. "You might even see a batch hatching."

Taryn sat straighter. "Really?"

She'd seen a turtle nest hatching on YouTube. The sand had bubbled then a circle overflowed with tiny flippers and shells pushing themselves out into the world. A nest was supposed to contain from fifty to over two hundred eggs. Now *that* was a big family.

"Throw a blanket out high on the beach and you might get lucky," the woman said, setting down the carafe. "But don't use a torch or flashlight. That confuses hatchlings." Swinging back her heavy fall of brunette hair, she again gestured down the beach. "You'll see the nests. The children mark them off."

Cole seemed interested, too. "You really think we might see some hatch?"

"Female turtles like to return to the same nesting ground, and that section is popular." After the woman had replaced used plates for clean, she ended, "Don't forget a blanket. Sea breezes can be cool at night."

As the woman headed off, Taryn sized Cole up. "So you like turtles, huh?"

"Tate's grade is signed up in some conservation program about them."

"Hopefully we'll get lucky and snap some close-up shots he can take to class." She pushed back her chair. "Think I might take the opportunity to catch up with that woman and get her ideas on other spots to check out while we're here."

"You'll find me on hammock duty."

As he got to his feet, too, and stretched those magnificent arms at angles above his head, Taryn pressed her lips together then said it anyway. He looked so striking yet relaxed. So unlike his usual blustering self.

"Maybe you shouldn't take a real vacation. It might feel so good, you'd never want to come back."

"Leave someone else in charge permanently?" Intentional or not, his fingers brushed hers as he passed. "Dream on."

"I've got blankets."

Cole glanced over from where he lay, swaying, half-asleep. Taryn stood a few feet away on the verandah, a stack of blankets in her arms. Rousing himself, he rocked out of the hammock onto his feet.

"Was that an invitation?" he asked.

"You said you liked turtles."

"I said Tate liked them." But, seriously, who didn't like turtles? He moved closer. "You won't be disappointed if nothing happens?"

"But something *might* happen."

Taking in the confident curve of her grin and—in that pink cotton slip of a dress—her other curves, too, he had to agree. *Something might happen,* and not just on the turtle front. But did he really want to put them both in that situation…alone on a secluded beach for an undefined amount of time, and with bedcoverings to boot?

Taking the blankets, Cole supposed the answer was an unconditional yes.

A few moments later, they were wandering down the beach with a full moon hanging high in its starry night sky.

"That woman was telling me how well this island does through visitors like us," she said. "They have a joint council and apparently invest the revenue wisely."

"Maybe they should spend some on decent public transportation and fixing up that welcome sign."

"Oh, Cole, it's all part of the charm. If you've stayed at one five-star, you've stayed at them all. But you'll never forget that taxi ride."

He winced. "Neither will my shoulder."

They came across a spot where a number of thigh-high stakes were erected and red tape wound around the wood. Protected areas for turtle nests.

Cole surveyed the surrounds—gently sloping dunes, soft sand, idyllic view. He laid out one of the blankets. "Looks like this is our base."

The blanket-covered dune made for one very comfortable backrest. Reclined side by side, he cast the other blanket over Taryn's bare legs. That woman was right. He found the breeze off the water refreshing, but Taryn might think it cool.

After several minutes of listening to water wash on the shore and foliage clattering behind them, he asked, "What do you think would be their favorite time to break out? Don't babies usually come around two in the morning?"

The breeze caught her soft laugh and carried it away. "Can you imagine them all asleep safe in their shells waiting for the right moment? And so many of them." She frowned. "Do you think mother turtles ever wonder how their babies make out?"

He grinned to assure her. "No, I don't."

Her gaze dropped and grew distant, then she said, "I wonder how Muffin and her big belly are holding up."

In the mix of moonlight and shadows, Taryn looked so thoughtful, he wanted to reach over and squeeze her hand for support, even if her concern was only over a cat.

"She'll be okay." Remembering her philosophy on strays wanting a home, he asked, "Have you got families picked out for the litter?"

"Are you interested?" She gave a playful smirk. "Oh, that's right. Real men don't own cats."

"I do like the fact they can look after themselves. Independent characters."

"There's no better feeling than knowing you can make your own way in life."

"So you don't dream of marrying a rich man who'll shower you with every luxury for the rest of your decadent life?"

"Guess you've met a few women who want to settle down with a wealthy tycoon slash tyrant."

He pretended to preen a tie. "Gee, you make me sound like such a catch."

She surrendered to a smile. "To answer your question, no. I've never wanted to marry for money."

"Me, either," he quipped.

"*If* you ever had the time to marry."

"Perhaps I'd make time if the right person came along."

When her eyes widened and suddenly neither of them had anything to say, Cole wished he'd thought before he'd come out with something that had sounded like a bad pickup line. He didn't use pickup lines—good, bad or anything in-between.

She jerked upright and looked ahead. "Was that some movement?"

He glanced around. "Not that I saw."

She reclined back, pulling the blanket extra high on her neck.

Cole exhaled. He really had made her uncomfortable. Best to let that thread drop and talk about something else. Something nonpersonal. But, truth was, he *wanted* to get personal. Whether it was the moon or the water or maybe even that delicious pink nectar, another twenty-four-plus hours alone with Taryn didn't seem long enough.

He picked up grains of sand and, in their silence, let them fall.

"I've made you anxious."

Still looking dead ahead, she shrugged. "Why would I be anxious?"

Oh, maybe because you're alone on a secluded beach with a man you want to kiss and who also wants to kiss you. Because earlier you'd gotten away with convincing yourself that you shouldn't—we shouldn't—when you know deep in your blood that we should.

"I'm not anxious," she went on. "I'm not…anything."

He mulled for a moment. Studied her profile.

"You're not."

She was winding her fingers deeper into the blanket, lifting the cover higher still around her neck. "Not in the least."

"And if I were to do this?"

He leaned toward her but stopped a heartbeat before his mouth met the sweep of her neck…when she'd be able to feel the warmth of his breath on her skin. "Are you anxious now?"

He heard her swallow. "That's not the word that springs to mind."

"Maybe we shouldn't worry about words." Giving in to the tide, he breathed in her intoxicating scent then brushed his lips over a pulse that beat erratically at the side of her throat. He felt her quiver, almost heard her questioning her own resolve. But she didn't bawl him out. Didn't move away.

Rather, still looking ahead, she lifted her chin and said, "I think we should go back."

"Anything you want." His lips brushed a line up to her lobe. *Anything at all.*

Her neck rocked slowly back. He imagined her eyes drifting shut…the hormones in her system heating and sparking just like his own.

Gently he turned her head until they were gazing into each other's eyes, noses touching. She quivered, but not from the cold.

"Would it surprise you to know," he said, "that I've always wanted to make love on a beach under a full moon with a batch of turtles ready to hatch?"

A smile touched her eyes. "What a coincidence."

He twirled his nose around hers, stole a featherlight kiss from one side of her mouth.

"Cole, when I said something might happen, I didn't mean this."

His hand on her arm, he brought her closer.

"I did."

Thirteen

Cole had said they shouldn't worry about words. As he drew her close and his mouth took hers, Taryn couldn't help but agree. The time for talk and gibes and delays was over. When she'd said she hadn't thought this would happen, she'd lied, and not only to Cole. She'd lied to herself.

All barriers needed to be lifted. No matter the reason for them being here, neither of them was able to escape the fact that they were attracted to each other—sexually, intellectually. On every level she could think of, she found Cole…intriguing.

Make that irresistible.

And as she pressed into his heat and accepted his kiss, that was all her mind could grasp and hold on to. He may be mulish; there were times she'd like to grab his shoulders and shake. He could irritate her. Goad her. At the same time, he stimulated her so often and so deeply, there was a part of her that had begun to crave the sound of his laugh, the slant of his smile. The incredible way he made her feel inside and out.

She drove her hands up through his hair, letting him know he didn't have to stop. He could kiss her harder, if he wanted. The physical flesh-on-flesh pleasure he stirred up within her… the heady, almost desperate feelings that followed… People may have been making love since the dawn of time, but never like this. If the world were to end in an hour, she wouldn't care, as long as she spent these last moments here, with Cole, like this.

Cole had flicked open his shirt buttons and was rolling out one shoulder and then angling while he shucked out of the other. When the rock-hard breadth of his chest brushed her bodice, her body instantly responded, her breasts swelling and nipples hardening to tight aching points.

Running out of air, she broke their kiss long enough to suck down a breath then clutch the hem of her dress. His gaze dark and hungry, Cole reached to help. While he grabbed the fabric rumpled around her thighs, she lifted up and raised both arms. She wiggled, he wrenched, and a moment later she was naked from her panties up.

His gaze filling hers, he crowded her back until she lay against the blanket-covered dune again. Then his head lowered, his mouth covered the peak of one breast and his tongue began to twirl. When his teeth nipped twice quickly, a bolt of shimmering lightning ripped through her veins.

Groaning in her throat, she held on to his head as her own rocked to one side and she arched up to soak in as much of this heaven as she could. His palm had molded over her other exposed breast, tracing and tickling the bead in an expert, mind-bending way. As her hands knotted in his hair then trailed to knead either side of his broad steamy back, she trembled with an overwhelming carnal need. She had to discover *all* of him. Every inch. Every shape and line.

He was kissing her again, his palm ironing down her belly, in beneath the elastic of her panties. When he reached the feminine crease between her legs, he sighed into her mouth. It felt as if his every muscle relaxed and then contracted extra tight. As he murmured something against her lips, a phrase about how beautiful she was—how much he'd looked for-

ward to this moment—a more cynical Taryn might think that
those were the kinds of things men said when they made love
to a woman. But in a place she trusted more, she knew that
he meant it. And right now she felt beautiful. Beautiful and
about to go up in flames!

She fumbled to grip the waistband of his jeans. Grinning
against her mouth, he let her struggle while his fingertip rose
up and down her swollen cleft. The crotch of her panties was
soaked and he seemed intent on only making her wetter. Dabbing soft moist kisses on her chin, her cheek, on each side of
her mouth, he drove a slow, burning circle around and over
her clit. She couldn't contain the tremors…the soul-deep sighs.
She wanted that smoldering bliss to go on and on, but she also
wanted to feel and experience him.

"Take off your jeans," she told him.

He stole another penetrating kiss then assured her, "Soon,
sweetheart, soon."

He shifted down, his lips trailing the slope of her neck,
the aching mounds of her breasts then over her ribs and her
ticklish belly. When he reached her navel, his tongue rode the
same captivating circle his finger now drew. In her mind's eye,
she saw his head working in a tight deliberate ring while the
circling down below grew tighter, too.

Her shoulders hunching up, she reflexively pushed his head
down. The next moment, the pressure of his finger was replaced by the adoring swirl of his tongue. Taryn gasped back a
breath and when the precursor rain of stars settled, she began
to move, her hips coaxed by his rhythm, her heart pounding
in time to that constant pulsing beat.

Bit by bit, the factions of light building in every quadrant
of her body began to glow brighter, and the heat condens-
ing at her core smoldered to a point where any moment, she
would catch on fire. Absorbing it all, she pressed down and
into herself, her eyes clamped shut, her breathing labored. She

thought he might back off a little, stop and start as a way of drawing her out. One half of her wanted him to do precisely that, while the other half dug in her claws and worked harder to find release.

Her hips moved faster. Biting her lip, she willed the looming orgasm to peak and break. Then, at the same time his mouth covered her completely and he began to lightly suck, she felt her lips eased apart and a long strong finger slip inside of her. When he applied the right amount of pressure to precisely the right place, a whirlpool of sensations flew together and magically fused. For a heartbeat, all feeling and thought were suspended, hovering in some far-off twilight universe. Then the explosion hit, shards flew out and a series of high fierce waves rocked every cell in her body.

Cole wasn't surprised her climax had come so quickly, that it was so intense. As much as he'd been driven by pure instinct these past few minutes, so had she, and the reward was complete immersion. Total release.

He'd loved the feel of his lips covering hers. He'd hardened to a brick when he'd tasted her breasts. But when his tongue had come in contact with this private slice of heaven, he hadn't known if he'd be able to hold off from ripping her panties completely off and, without patience or apology, driving his erection home. Given all the signals, she had wanted him inside of her that way, too.

But he'd held off, enjoying beyond belief giving her this pleasure. Now that it had come, he wanted to prolong her peak as long as possible. If his shaft hadn't been pounding away, he'd have happily stayed here all night doing only this. And as he withdrew his finger and felt just how intense her orgasm must have been, it was natural that he'd want to enjoy that, too. He nudged her thighs wider apart and settled his lips an inch or so lower. Her scent, mixed with that flavor, was wonderfully earthy yet intoxicatingly sweet.

Enjoying her this way, he felt the last of her contractions squeeze and pulse until, reaching to rub her fingers through his hair, Taryn hummed in her throat and urged him up.

Face-to-face again, she looked into his eyes and her slumberous gaze said it all. His lips wet with the taste of her, he traced them over hers then kissed her, at first very softly then more and more deeply. At the same time, he maneuvered until he was free of the rest of his clothes.

He always carried his wallet in his back pocket. Now he broke the kiss only long enough to find one of the foil wraps he kept inside the zipped section.

Spread out on their blanket, she reached her arms to him at the same time he moved to position himself. As her thighs wrapped around the back of his, he kissed her again and the engorged head of his erection pierced and at last entered her. Her head went back as she sucked in a breath while he clenched his jaw and every tendon in his body locked tight.

When he had the pressure under control, he began to move, his mind drifting, floating, as he filled more and more of her and his own sensations climbed.

He pushed up onto elbows and, eyes closed, drilled ever deeper while Taryn's fingers fanned over his chest and the bulging cords in his neck. Even though he knew there would definitely be a next time, and soon, he wanted this to last… the throbbing, pushing burn, the heavenly slide of her body beneath his. But the fire was too hot. His need for release too great. As he craned his neck toward the moon, she held on to his arms and he pumped a final mind-blowing time.

Fourteen

"Doesn't Australia seem a long way away?"

Taryn and Cole were lying together under the stars. The moon had dropped halfway into the ocean and everything was spookily quiet—as if the whole world were asleep.

Except for them.

Cuddling closer into the heat of his hard chest, she replied, "Doesn't sound as if you're in a hurry to get back."

"I feel strangely at ease." His lips nuzzled her hair. "Wonder why."

Because they'd just made love. But even in her mind, that sounded way too simple. Yes, their bodies had joined, but she felt as if their spirits had met, too. This was what being with someone was supposed to feel like. Totally absorbing. Completely fulfilling. Wondering how she'd ever find the wherewithal to move from this divine spot and leave this time behind, she snuggled in more.

Whether Cole felt as moved by the experience as she did, Taryn couldn't say. Nor would she ask. She might be feeling all wistful and in love with the universe. But more than instinct said Cole, or any man for that matter, didn't want to come over all marshmallow, dissecting feelings composed mainly of postcoital buzz…with feeling unbelievably fulfilled on every level. Rather he might like to broaden the discussion. Probably not such a bad idea.

"There's another reason you'd feel more relaxed. Your father's troubles are sorted."

He was quiet for a long time, simply stroking her arm with two fingers.

"I was thinking about my mother earlier today," he finally said. "Do you know she used to call me special?"

Taryn smiled. "I'm sure you were."

"She said I was so brave and clever, I was bound to grow into a man everyone could rely on."

"And you're living up to her prediction."

"Yeah. I'm the fix-it guy."

"What do you think would happen if you didn't run yourself ragged trying to fix everything all the time?"

Now that she'd seen him a league away from the office, unburdened like this, she couldn't help but wonder.

"If I didn't keep an eye on Hunter's dealings in the States as well as back home, frankly, I'd run the risk of seeing it all fall apart."

"Is it really that bad?"

"Let's just say, it's a full-time job."

"And the price you pay is a coronary."

"I got the impression you were a 'dot every i' type, too. I'm still not convinced you didn't order one bedroom, even subconsciously."

She knuckled his ribs. "You're not that good."

"Aren't I?"

He drew her up so that she lay on top of him. Then he kissed her, tenderly and with infinite meaning…in a way he hadn't kissed her before. And all the problems and doubts in the world faded clean away.

When they came up for air, she breathed out a long sigh then lay her cheek on his shoulder.

"Well, on second thought," she said, "maybe you are that good."

When Taryn woke in bed the next morning, the sun had just peeked over the horizon and the sheet-rumpled space beside her was empty.

Sitting up with a start, she pushed back hair fallen over her brow then relaxed, remembering how her evening with Cole had ended. The most romantic night of her life.

After making love again on the beach and coming to terms with the fact that no baby turtles were likely to hatch, they'd meandered back to the bungalow. Sandy and sticky, they'd showered together—soaping each other up then taking their sweet time to wash each other down. After drying off, they'd jumped into this bed and, with that rattan fan beating warm air over their heads, had continued to talk and kiss and more.

What time had she fallen asleep? Didn't matter. She'd never felt more refreshed. And disappointed. She'd imagined cuddling up with Cole this morning and repeating what had unfolded atop that blanket the night before, and possibly exploring other pleasure points, too…finding more ways to please. Then again, she couldn't envision feeling any more satisfied. The problem was she wanted more.

Wanted *now*.

So much it frightened her a little.

As she found her negligee wrap, Taryn wondered. Perhaps she would live to regret this coming together. Cole Hunter was first and foremost her boss, after all. Carrying on from that, he was committed to his company—to his family—and had no room for anything or anyone else in his life. Any woman foolish enough to entertain flowery notions about a lasting relationship with a man like that was headed for trouble.

Thoughtful, she knotted her wrap's sash and wandered out to the main room.

Trouble. Yes, Cole was certainly that. But he was also exciting and sexy and, dammit, she was going to take this unexpected, wonderful moment in time for what it was. A thrilling, soul-lifting one-off. Once they were back home, the involvement no doubt would end. Because nothing screwed with a girl's career more than trying to negotiate an office affair.

A good friend had walked down that long dark road and had come out losing everything on the other side—job, self-respect, pretty much her sanity. Taryn had quietly deemed herself too smart to fall into that trap.

But this slip with Cole didn't need to be fatal. It was like having one bad day on a diet. Come day after tomorrow, she'd simply correct her course, get back on the bike and wean herself off him. Difficult, but doable.

From a bowl on the coffee table, she grabbed a banana and, peeling the skin, made her way toward the larger entrance of the bungalow, which invited in a panoramic view of the bay. Biting into the fruit, she surveyed the near surrounds but Cole was nowhere to be seen. Perhaps he'd hooked up with that sweet boy.

She crossed over to the kitchenette. While pouring some chilled nectar, she eyed her laptop sitting on the counter. Those pictures and videos she shot yesterday were waiting to be downloaded. Roman had made her promise she'd take loads. He wanted to see them all.

Roman was an intuitive type, Taryn decided. Would he pick up on the changed vibe between her and Cole? What would he think of the situation—of her—if he discovered she'd slept with the one man who decided whether her show made the cut?

A flash of guilt gripped her stomach, but right now Taryn only wanted to embrace feeling good. She wanted to remember the way Cole's mouth and hands had moved over her body like an artist's, creating sensations and bringing out emotions she hadn't thought existed.... Standing here alone, naked beneath this filmy wrap, she felt helpless not to close her eyes and conjure up more memories, more bone-melting must-have-again moments.

When Taryn opened her eyes, her gaze landed on an item lying on the main table—a flower. Massive and scarlet in color, it looked so perfect, Taryn wondered if it were fake. Crossing over, she ran two fingertips across a satin-soft petal. She could check on the video she'd taken of this room not long after they'd arrived, but she was certain it hadn't been here then. And no one else had been inside this room since that man had dropped off their luggage.

Had Cole brought this flower home for her this morning? Beneath it all, was he that romantic?

She'd assumed Cole would want this interlude to be short and sweet. He was an astute businessman with little time for R & R, not a man to be led by his heart. But did she have it wrong? He had dropped a hint once, hadn't he? Was Cole Hunter truly looking for the right person? The right woman?

Not that she wanted to be that woman necessarily. She was a career person. Foremost, at this time in her life, she wanted her show to air and succeed.

But maybe this island truly could work miracles. Make people rethink who they were and why they were here on this earth.

Outside, footfalls sounded on the steps. The next minute, Cole's masculine frame filled the doorway. He was wet, rubbing a towel down his face, over his slick dark hair. His bare chest pumping after what Taryn guessed had been a jog up from the beach, he saw her and broke into a smile that left her heart thudding all the more. Would he present her with the gorgeous flower now?

Moving forward, he brushed a cool kiss across her cheek

and stayed close to drawl, "I was hoping you'd still be in bed." He drew back a little. "I couldn't resist the idea of a swim."

"I can't resist you."

Bouncing up on her toes, she snatched a kiss a moment before a hungry smile swam up in his gorgeous green eyes. Dropping the towel, he wound his big cool arms around her.

"That felt like an invitation."

"I figure it's too early for work."

His focus had dropped to her neck, to the slope of flesh that led to one shoulder. The cold tip of his index finger eased her wrap away from the spot before his head lowered. She sighed as his mouth lightly sucked then nibbled then sucked again.

He murmured against her skin, "You taste good."

"And I have it on good authority that's not the best part."

She tugged the tie at her waist, shucked back her shoulders and the wrap joined his towel on the floor.

With firm intent, his hands slid lower, over her backside, as his wet shorts pressed unashamedly against her belly. He was already hard and she was keen to make him harder.

"I'd better warn you," he said. "I'm ravenous in the morning."

She coiled her arms around his neck. "You're always hungry."

His playful gaze darkened to a more serious hue as he concentrated on her lips. "So feed me."

He carried her back to that bed where they stayed, and played, until well after ten when his cell on the dresser beeped. He hesitated, clearly wondering who was after him now, before he resumed tickling her nipple with the tip of his very skilled tongue.

Bodily exhausted, but passions still switched on to high, she ran a hand over the back of his head, through his tousled dark hair.

"You don't want to see who that is?"

He switched to her other breast. "Nope."

Sighing, she arched up as his tongue twirled one way around the peak then the other.

"It might not be work related," she said dreamily.

"It's work related."

"Might be family."

"Like I said…"

"Might be Tate."

She felt him smile. "Tate isn't allowed to use the phone."

"Guess he is a little young."

"But smart. He knows his own home number. Mine, too."

Moving up, he curled an arm around her head and asked, "When did your aunt trust you with a phone of your own?"

"I got one when I started a part-time job during senior year in high school. It was the first thing I bought with a wage. No. Second. I'd had my eye on a cream silk dress for weeks."

"What was the third thing?"

"I saved up and gave some money to an agency to help find someone from my past."

Tipping on his side, he rested his weight on his elbow. Finally he asked, "Your father?"

"Mother. My father abandoned us before I was born. My mother bowed out later when I was a tot. If it hadn't been for Vi, I wouldn't have had an opinion on family worth voicing. She's supportive and understanding, and she saved me from feeling worse about my childhood than I should.

"I remember," she went on, "when I was maybe only five or six, Vi dated a man with kind smiling eyes and a belly laugh that filled the house. I thought they'd be together forever and I'd get the mob of brothers and sisters I wanted. But they broke up. I remember finding my aunt sometimes trying to cover her tears." Taryn had spilled a few tears of her own.

Cole seemed to take that all in before he asked, "Did the agency find her?"

"Yep. I even went to see her. She was living with a bunch of people on the coast of Northern New South Wales. My aunt said she'd come with me, but I wanted to do it on my own."

"Was it a happy reunion?"

"Actually it was a huge letdown. She tried to make out like she was glad to see me, then she came up with a ton of excuses why she'd needed to leave me behind. She never stopped fidgeting, acting cornered. Just one of those women who should never have had children, I guess. But I'm glad I went. We even swapped emails for a time. When she died a few years later, I went to the funeral. Paid for a headstone. Would you believe she wanted to be buried with a bottle of rum?"

He drew in closer and held her gaze with his. "She missed out."

"I've thought about organizing to have flowers put on her grave each anniversary of her death, but I can't bear to think of them sitting there, week after week, all withered and brown. I should probably go plant a rosebush or something. Not sure if that's allowed."

But she'd talked enough about the past. She wanted to get back those other, happy feelings.

Winding a finger through a lock of hair that had fallen over his brow, she said, "By the way, I like the flower you brought back for me this morning."

"Flower?"

"The red hibiscus. It's as big as a plate." When he frowned, she went on. "You left it on the table, remember?"

"Oh, that. No. That boy with the bucket brought it back from the spring yesterday. He must have ducked in to leave it there for you. It was closed up, asleep, when we found it."

Taryn blinked then said, "Oh," and forced an easy smile. "I just assumed it was you. Doesn't matter."

But deep down, it stung a little. Made her feel foolish for thinking he'd gone to the trouble.

Which meant she was getting way too caught up here. Yes, they'd slept together—a number of times in only a few hours. The day they'd met, Cole had suggested she may have had an affair with her former boss, which she'd denied, and she felt he'd believed her. But did he wonder about that now? Or did he see this experience for what it was? A once-in-a-lifetime fling between two consenting adults who happened to work together. It wasn't ideal but it happened. It had happened to *them*.

And thinking of it that way only reinforced that she had no reason to come over all adolescent now. He didn't give her that flower. Didn't matter. No big deal.

He was studying her neck, sliding a fingertip around the décolletage.

"You don't wear a chain," he said.

"I have a pile of costume jewelry," she said, her thoughts preoccupied now.

"But nothing that says Tiffany?"

"Their pieces are beautiful, but I'm not a jewelry kind of girl." She was a *flower* kind of girl.

He looked at her for a long moment as if debating something in his head…like maybe how he would handle this situation when they got back? How he would go about closing the door. Perhaps with a parting gift. A piece of jewelry. She'd already accepted that what had happened between them was never meant to last. And yet as that feeling of preoccupation turned into unease, suddenly she knew they'd spent enough time in bed. They needed to start moving. Get back to reality. To work. She'd mentioned it earlier so Cole knew that her video camera was charged, ready for a shoot involving that volcano.

He must have sensed or seen her change in mood because, tipping back, he said the words for her.

"Perhaps we should get on with our day."

"I think that's a good call."

Without another word, he slid out from beneath the sheets and, naked, headed for the adjoining bathroom. But Taryn lay there a moment longer, going over in her mind the past few minutes. She didn't accept expensive gifts. She didn't want them. But believing that he'd brought a flower back here for her…

A simple thought like that would have meant so much.

When he came out from the shower, into the main room, Taryn was moving away from the table. He saw that flower lying there. She'd said it had been as large as a plate, but now, again, all the petals were closed.

"Did you get your message?" she asked, moving to her laptop, which sat on the kitchen counter.

"Message?" he asked.

"Your phone beeped again. Twice."

He rubbed his brow, dragging his hand down his face. It was a gorgeous Saturday morning. He was on a picturesque Pacific isle with a woman who made love like a goddess and, ten minutes ago, had again put up her wall. Because he'd hinted at giving her a gift? Well, that was one for the books. Or was there something he wasn't seeing?

He returned to the bedroom and slid his cell off the dresser. Three recent messages. All from his father.

After he'd listened to the first, he didn't need to hear the rest. Didn't need to feel any sicker. Angrier. When he got hold of Jeremy Judge, by God, he'd throw him down on the ground and—

"Business?"

He glanced up. Taryn stood at the doorway, her long fair

hair loose and hanging over bare shoulders. She wore a strappy lime-green dress that complemented her skin tone. Her gaze was bright but also very much back to reserved. He stabbed the redial key. He didn't have time for holding hands now.

"There's been another attempt on my father's life."

Her breath caught. "That can't be."

"I'll get Brandon front and center on the case straightaway," he said to himself, fast dialing then grabbing his bag off the floor, dumping it on rumpled sheets then striding into the bathroom to collect his gear, all with the cell pressed to his ear.

For God's sake, pick up!

"Does that mean that other man, the man who died, wasn't responsible?" she asked. "Or that he wasn't working—"

"How the hell should I know?"

Storming out from the bathroom, he was confronted by Taryn's wounded gaze. Oh, hell. He so didn't need this right now. Neither did he want to act like a brute.

He left a quick urgent message for Brandon then took one step toward her. "Look, I'm sorry. It's just…" He shut his eyes and cursed at himself. "I should *never* have left."

"What could you have done?"

"What I should have done from the start. Taken charge. And to hell if someone didn't like it."

"Meaning your father."

"Meaning anyone on God's green earth."

He shoved his toothbrush and aftershave in his bag then drove a hand in to drag out a clean pair of trousers.

"You're leaving?" she asked.

"Soon as I can."

"There's no connecting flight out until this afternoon."

"Then I'll organize a private flight."

He stepped into his chinos. Pulled out a tee. He heard her question as if from afar.

"Cole, what happened?"

"Two men clubbed my father. When a bystander rushed up to help, they almost managed to shove Tate into their van. I would never have forgiven myself if…"

His stomach pitched. Dammit, he wanted to hit something. Break it in two and hit it again.

"Cole, this isn't your fault."

"Someone else started this, but, by God, I'll finish it."

Driving the shirt on over his head, he noticed Taryn at the wardrobe, dragging out her own bag. He frowned.

"What are you doing?"

"I'm going with you."

"This isn't your fight."

"You need someone with you."

"I've never needed anyone."

"Everyone needs someone, Cole."

Something shifted deep inside of him, but he pushed it aside and reminded her, "That volcano's expecting you and your camera."

"Guess the volcano will have to wait."

"But this survey, your show—"

"Are important. But this takes priority."

He held her gaze then, remembering the clock was ticking, he turned to find his shoes.

She went over and held his hand. When he met her gaze again, she asked, "Is your dad okay?"

After a tense moment, he blew out a breath.

"He's at home, resting."

"And Tate?"

With his free hand, Cole held his throbbing head. "There are some crazy sons of bitches out there. People who don't have a moment's hesitation in hurting someone who can't defend themselves. Tate's all right. I'm going to make sure he stays that way."

"What is it you think they want?"

"Always comes down to money, doesn't it?"

"A ransom. But I thought these were attempts on your father's life. A ransom demand's no good if you don't have a bargaining chip."

His stomach tightened before it rolled over twice. He murmured, "I have this horrible feeling…"

"What?"

"That Eloise is connected to this in some way."

"Guthrie's wife? Trying to kill him? Why on earth would she want to do that? He must treat her like a queen."

"Women like Eloise are never satisfied." He remembered the way she'd come on to him—Guthrie's oldest son—whenever they were alone, and the sick feeling in his stomach grew ten times worse. He grabbed his cell again.

"I need to make a couple of phone calls. To organize that private flight first off…"

"And the second call?"

"Jeremy Judge." He scowled. "I'm looking forward to firing his ass."

Fifteen

What had gotten into her?

How had she ever summoned the nerve to tell Cole that not only was she leaving on that private flight off the island with him, but she was also tagging along when he confronted his family about these ongoing attempts on his father's life?

Now, hours later, Cole pulled his car up in front of the Hunter mansion. Taryn told herself again: there was no reason for her being here, other than the one she'd already given. After the intimate time they'd shared, brief though it had been, she cared about him. She cared about Guthrie and little Tate, too. She wanted to help if she could, even if help only meant offering her support.

Call her curious, but she also wanted to meet Eloise Hunter.

Cole hadn't elaborated on his suspicions—that he believed his father's second wife was involved in these assassination attempts against Guthrie. But there must be some good reason for Eloise to have created such a big blip on his radar. Taryn assumed no one else knew of his concerns, least of all Guthrie. How would his father react if his would-be killer turned out to be the woman who had pledged to love him till death us do part?

But Taryn knew better than most. Some people didn't give a rat's behind about the people they should care most about.

Taryn sympathized with Cole. The Hunter family was indeed a tangled web. How must he feel being the "special one," feeling responsible for trying to keep all the spiders out?

Cole opened her passenger-side door and she followed as he strode up a half dozen wide granite steps to the massive front doors. Before she'd caught up, he'd rung the bell twice. Now he was thumping the panels with the side of one fist. When a woman—obviously staff—responded to the ruckus, Cole seemed less impressed than he had been all day.

The woman said, "Are Mr. and Mrs. Hunter expecting you?"

Cole all but pushed the woman out of his way. He was halfway across the huge shining foyer when he stopped, turned and held out his hand, waiting for her before he charged on.

Absorbing her surrounds, Taryn took his hand and followed. The grounds of the estate were impressive enough. Pristine manicured lawns with soaring pines delineating an endless paved drive. Inside, however, Taryn was left near speechless. Everything screamed wealth. Extravagant embroidered furnishings. Magnificent art hanging from towering walls. The room they'd entered was larger than a regular-sized city apartment. The cost of maintaining this grandeur must be exorbitant.

Guthrie was resting on a couch, gazing out a window that took in a one-eighty-degree view of a back lawn that presented more like a state garden. Guthrie looked over as they entered but he didn't get to his feet. One leg rested on cushions on the couch and a square bandage sat high on the right side of his forehead.

Cole came straight to the point. "I fired your wonder P.I."

"Jeremy told me that you called." Guthrie swiveled a little

and spotted his other guest. "Taryn, sorry to call you away early from your work."

Feeling horrible for the whole situation, she edged forward. "Are you all right?"

Guthrie touched his head. "A bruise here and there. My pride's wounded the most. If not for that man who'd been walking his dog, I can't say where we'd be now."

Cole asked, "Where's Tate?"

"In the media room with a policeman standing guard. Son, I wonder whether we should put Tate somewhere safe until this is over."

"Safe like where?"

"Perhaps with one of your brothers. Whatever madman we're dealing with here, hopefully he won't have connections that far abroad."

"Let's get Brandon in on this first," Cole said, "then we can nut out what needs to be done."

At that moment, a fourth person entered the room. Taryn recognized the face from media shots and the photo Guthrie kept on his desk. Eloise Hunter was of medium height and svelte, other than a baby bump. Wearing a black silk-and-chiffon pantsuit straight out of the pages of Vogue, she looked as if she were attending a celebrity wake. Only no one was dead. God willing, it would stay that way.

Taryn expected the mistress of the house to be either overly gracious to her or serve up a cursory glance; she was, after all, no one of consequence. But on seeing Taryn, Eloise stopped in her tracks and, without regard to social etiquette, eyed her up and down as if *she* might have been a person who intended her family harm.

Taryn bristled. Within five seconds of meeting Mrs. Hunter, she understood Cole's disapproval. What happened next made her hackles rise more. Eloise's focus slid away from her and settled upon the younger of the Hunter men present. The glimmer in those amber eyes was unmistakable. Eloise found her stepson physically attractive. She might be running her fingers up and down the side of the water glass she held but in her mind, her hand was stroking something far more personal.

Apparently unaware, Guthrie took care of introductions. "Darling, this is Taryn Quinn, a producer we've put on."

Eloise's gaze flicked back and a meaningless smile curved her lips. But then a wiser glint shone in her eyes and she focused again on Cole. It took all Taryn's restraint not to save Eloise the trouble of guessing and admit out loud that, yes, she and Cole were lovers. And that was the *second* reason Eloise needed to keep those restless paws to herself.

Another guest entered the room. Beside her, Cole stiffened and braced. She heard him mutter, *"Judge.*

"What are you doing here?" Cole spoke to the man. "I said we were done."

"I take my orders from the elder Mr. Hunter," the man— Judge—said, lacing his hands before him. "And unless he's changed his mind in the past five minutes, I'm still on the payroll."

Cole growled. "How did you get things so wrong? Where were you when my father was bashed and my brother nearly kidnapped?"

"I understand you're upset—"

"You know nothing about me."

"I have a father, too," Judge pressed on. "A man I respect and would give my life for. Instead of locking horns, Cole, let's work together to put the people responsible away."

Cole looked set to pounce when Guthrie cut in.

"Cole, you have my blessing to bring Brandon in. Tell him he can have anything he needs. But on one condition. He works with Jeremy. He did, after all, save my life that night."

As if she were oblivious to it all, Eloise sidled up closer to Cole. "It's been a long day. Need a drink?"

Cole grunted, "What I need is a club."

Regardless of injury, Guthrie got to his feet. "That's enough, son. Nothing more can be done here today. Go home. We'll talk again tomorrow."

Cole lifted his chin. "I'm seeing Tate before I go."

He took Taryn's hand and, plowing on past Judge, led her through that room, down a long corridor and up a level where they finally entered a room without knocking.

A uniformed man stood inside the door. Now one hand flew to his holster. Taryn covered her mouth to smother the gasp while, at the center of the room, a young fair-haired boy turned his head. Tate's face burst into a deep-dimpled smile. He threw down his game controller and ran full speed up to them. He flung out his arms at the same time Cole scooped him up and held him tight. Taryn thought she saw moisture at the corners of Cole's closed-tight eyes while the policeman answered a call on his two-way: Judge passing on to expect the eldest of the Hunter boys soon.

Still hugging Tate close, Cole's voice was thick when he asked, "How you doing, kiddo?"

"I got a scratch on my knee, Cole, but it doesn't hurt." Tate wound back and looked over. "Who are you?"

"I'm Taryn. It's good to meet you."

Tate spoke again to his big brother. "She's pretty. Are you staying for dinner?"

"Not tonight, chum." Cole set Tate down but stayed crouched so they could talk eye to eye. "There's no need to be scared, okay?"

"I'm not scared. Not anymore. But I still wish you could stay." Tate's mouth swung to one side then he leaned closer and whispered, "Daddy says I might get to fly over to see Dex or Wynn for a while."

"How do you feel about that?"

"Good, so long as it's Dex."

"Why Dex?"

"Coz he lives right near Disneyland and he's always saying on the phone he wants to take me."

Cole chuckled and in that moment Taryn felt a large measure of his tension drain away. Her aunt said that blood was always thicker than water. He might grumble about his brothers in California and New York, but Cole would trust them to look after the person he loved perhaps more than anyone in the world. That said a lot.

Cole ruffled Tate's hair. "Go finish your game."

"I'd better go wash up for dinner."

"You hungry?"

Tate beamed up. "I'm always hungry."

Laughing, Cole stooped to give Tate another bear hug then, together, she and Cole walked down that hall. But he didn't take the turn that led back to the sitting room they'd left. Instead they found their way out via another route. A couple of minutes later they were buckled up in his car, leaving the estate and its majesty behind.

His gaze on the road and mouth drawn tight, Cole said, "Thanks."

"What for?"

"For leaving the island to be here with me today. I know how much getting the most out of that survey meant to you."

Taryn was taken aback by the sincerity in his voice, by the vulnerability in his face. To save herself from sounding too moved, she almost quipped, *Sure. You owe me one.*

But she was happy she'd come and had witnessed firsthand the pressure Cole was under. She'd come out with an even broader understanding of his ingrained sense of commitment. To everyone.

As far as her being here for him was concerned, he didn't owe her a thing.

* * *

When Cole pulled up in her drive, Taryn didn't have to ask
ask him inside. He must know that she wanted him to spend
the night and although he was understandably on edge, she
knew he wanted to be with her, too.

He carried her bag into the bedroom then, standing in the
early evening's misty shadows, he turned to face her. For a moment, a flicker of some emotion she couldn't name shuttered
over his expression before a fated smile lifted one corner of
his mouth. Without a word, he reached for her and she came.

They didn't kiss. Not at first. He found the zip at the side of
her summer dress and eased it down at the same time as she
unbuttoned his shirt. After he'd slipped the dress off over her
head, she tipped forward and, breathing in his musky scent, let
her fingers roam over his pecs then higher to skim his pow-
erful shoulders. She slid the sleeves off his strong long arms
while he gazed down into her eyes, searching deeper than he
ever had before.

When she caught the button at his trouser's waistband, he
held her hand back then carefully dropped his head into the
sweep of her neck. As his teeth slow danced over the skin, her
every fiber ignited with a desire so pure, the sensations stole
her breath. His warm, slightly roughed palms drew arcs over
her bare back, up under her hair, and he murmured at her ear.

"I like when you don't wear a bra."

She quivered and sighed, pressing herself closer as pulsing heat drifted to converge in the lowest point in her belly.
His mouth was moving lower, too, tenderly drinking its way
across the curve of her collarbone as one hand moved to cup
and measure the weight of one breast.

"Don't wear them anymore," he said, obviously meaning
bras. "Not when you're with me."

The tip of his tongue slid up her neck, ran a line over her
parted lips, and as his fingers swooped around then lightly

pinched and rolled one burning nipple, she opened up more and welcomed him into her mouth.

Although she adored his foreplay, she was near desperate to have him on top, pushing inside of her. She needed that connection. She knew he needed it, too. She wanted to tell him just that, and in words that shouldn't be uttered in public. She needed him naked and she didn't care if it was on the bed, on the floor, pressed up hard against that dark cupboard wall. The time they'd already spent together making love had been intoxicating, but this minute she was fevered, burning up. That he'd begun to slide down against her body to his knees didn't help. These past hours had been so filled with concern. She'd missed the intimate feel of him, his scent, the thrill.

With his tongue trailing lower past her navel and a set of fingers hooking down into her panties' front, she let her neck rock back and the conflagration take over.

He parted her folds and kissed her with his lips then with his tongue. All the while he stayed with her nipple, rolling and gently extending the peak while his mouth circled that other ultrasensitive bead. His teeth nipped and tugged at the same time as she heard his deep groan of pleasure. He felt so strong whereas she was trembling, every thought she'd ever owned set aside to concentrate on the growing fire, the rhythmic rub of his jaw against her inner thighs.

Mind-blowing sparks began shooting through her blood. Her legs started to shake and nothing in the world mattered other than the fact that she hovered above and all around this excruciatingly sweet crescendo. She needed the release so badly, but she was already half out of her mind, and she wanted to do something new for them both.

She tried to shift away from his mouth, but the hand on her behind held her firm while his rhythm didn't miss a beat. Again she let herself be drawn toward that throbbing light before, grinning, she wedged a palm between his mouth and her mound and pried herself away.

In patches of thin light, she saw him glance up, his brow furrowed.

"But you like that," he said.

"I do."

"Well, I like it, too." He grinned. "In the work comes the reward."

She laughed but when his head went forward again, she wound away and climbed up onto the bed. His teeth flashed white on a smile. With a couple of deft moves, his trousers were down and kicked aside. He set something—she guessed a condom—on the bedside table and then he came to her, ready to resume where they'd left off. Instead of letting him take the lead, she pounced and drove him onto his back.

Craning up, he laughed. "Hey, you play rough."

"Is that a complaint?"

His back met the mattress again. "No, ma'am."

Leaving her panties on, she came closer and feathered her lips over his small flat nipples, down over his ribs. She dotted hungry openmouthed kisses in four spots around his navel. Then her head went down.

Grazing her nails over his scrotum, she held his shaft in her other hand and rolled the full length of her tongue around that hot rounded tip. Beside her head, his hand fisted into the coverlet as his hips arched up. Smiling to herself, she circumnavigated a few more times before, squeezing lightly, she slid farther down.

He throbbed in her mouth, and at the back of her throat she tasted a little of him…a tease of what was yet to come. His palm slid up over her shoulder to knead her nape as she moved and stroked, and his erection hardened more. Deep, maddeningly sexy sounds rumbled through his chest and body, vibrating over her lips and lower. He began to move and his strokes on the back of her head became more instinctive. Immersing herself in all her senses, she shifted until she was embedded between the V of his legs and he couldn't escape. She doubted he wanted to.

She'd thought she could handle him, but the width and thrust soon became too much. A moment before she could slide her lips away, perhaps reading the signs, he reached down to ease her up. He didn't roll her over but rather held her on top by gripping her high on the back of one thigh. Grabbing the condom, he rolled on protection then expertly pushed up and in. A rush of euphoria doused her inside and out. So many endorphins, she felt intoxicated…floating on a slipstream that was about to take her unbelievably high.

Her lips ran over the damp slide of his brow before she came away to look into his eyes as he smiled softly, moving and coaxing her sizzling fuse closer to that beautiful big bang. She was balanced, on the verge, when he held her cheek and whispered her name.

A heartbeat later, his erection drove in to the hilt, hitting that single perfect spot. As the orgasm took him, he squeezed her thigh, she let out a gasp and the universe contracted before blowing wide apart.

Sixteen

They spent Sunday together at her place, not working, not stressing. Just unwinding, her reading a novel, him watching sports on TV. Cole didn't think he'd ever enjoyed an entire day of doing nothing before. He felt guilty. Rested. A small part of him even felt at peace.

For the most part, however, he was thinking about Guthrie and Tate—how bad that day when Tate had almost been abducted could have turned out. Brandon had been brought into the loop. His father insisted that he keep Judge on the case, too. Nothing Cole could do about that. But he wanted those animals, and whoever was behind this whole sordid mess, found and appropriately dealt with. *Fast.*

The next day, Cole visited Taryn in her office. She said she'd get together what she could from the survey, given they'd been called away early. He said he needed a more definite budget projection. Then she asked whether she ought to start organizing host auditions. Between leaving her office and stealing a drugging hot kiss, Cole told her to hang off for now.

Tuesday night he spent over at her place. He watched on while she called for that cat to come in from the cold. Later they'd had pizza and watched a movie neither of them saw much of. Wednesday night Taryn stayed at his place. Thursday, he was back at hers and she was still calling in that stubborn pregnant cat. They'd had Chinese and he'd told her about the time the boys had built a cubby house in the backyard and it had collapsed with him inside. She'd been impressed by the scar on his shin caused during the cave-in by a dislodged dartboard.

By Friday, he was prickly over the fact Brandon and Judge had nothing new to report. However, Brandon passed on in private that, despite her many vices, Eloise was clear of any suspicion. That spooky maid was cleared, too. Come lunchtime, Cole was settled behind his desk, working on more tweaks to that massive, frustrating, football league contract, when Taryn swept into his office and put a pamphlet on his desk.

Grinning, Cole sat back. She was a cross between angelic and sexy in that crisp white linen dress that, to his mind, could have benefitted from an inch or two less length around the hem. Calculating back how many hours it had been since they'd last kissed—last made love—he collected the pamphlet and looked it over.

"What's this?" he asked.

"A new park opened not far from here." She came around to his side of the desk. Her perfume teasing his nostrils and testing his resistance in a work setting, she tapped a picture on the sheet. "There are paddleboats."

He nodded. "Okay."

Her blue eyes flashed and a big smile spread. "Then you'll come?"

"Come where? When?"

"To paddle with me. Now." She checked her wristwatch. "It's lunchtime. I vote foot-long hot dogs."

Shunting the pamphlet aside, he chuckled. Taryn was a mile away from the aloof woman he'd met three weeks ago. Of course, she would never lose that poise; a person either had class or she didn't. And, God knows, he would love to ditch and go play for a couple of hours. But he'd been slack all week. He'd even slid across some duties for Roman to take on full-time. But he couldn't hide forever from his responsibilities. He had an example to set.

"Sounds tempting," he said, "but I ought to get this contract sorted."

She leaned back against his desk's edge. Her palms set flat behind her, shoulders raised, her skirt lifted that ideal inch or two.

"The work will still be here when you get back," she reasoned with a silky tone, and he flicked a glance at the open office door. Maybe they could enjoy some hands-on time now without needing to leave the building.

After easing out of his chair, he stood before her then leaned in until his hard thighs pinned hers. His palms anchored on either side of hers on the desk, he closed his eyes, grazed his chin lightly up her cheek then murmured in her ear.

"I think we should lock the door."

When her hand came up and fingers twined through his hair, every pulse point in his body started to tick and, soon, throb.

"You spend too much time indoors," she told him while he tasted the satin curve of her neck. "Let's get some sunshine. It's a gorgeous day."

"And later?"

"Later you can finish with that contract."

He pressed in more. "What contract?"

She laughed. "You have some casual clothes here, don't you?"

As his hand slid over and scooped around her back, the best he could do was grunt his affirmative.

"I do, too," she said, then sighed. "We'll change, go paddle some boats and then…"

He drew back slightly. "Couldn't we do the 'and then' part first?"

She pushed against his chest and he let her shift him away. "I'll meet you in the lobby."

He took from those hypnotic lips a lingering kiss. "I'll be there in five."

They drove to the park. For a Friday—a workday—it was packed. Guess it was a combination of the good weather, he mused, a novel array of food vendors and the curiosity of a new place to take the kids. Or your lover.

He paid for thirty minutes in a paddleboat, but, willing to pay more and give their legs a fine workout, they spent an hour on the lake. If ever he thought about that contract, or his father, Cole told himself to chill. They were headed back to her place for the "and then" part, after which he'd get back on top of things, but when they were almost at her address, he decided to check his cell for messages. Just to be safe.

He had parked in her drive, which was looking quite familiar these days, and Taryn was already out and scooting up to open the front door. Cole opened his messages and was bombarded by a stream of recent texts and voice mail. As he went through, his gut sank lower and the sense of dread swelled until he wasn't certain he could breathe.

Liam had been trying to get him. He'd been offered a better deal with a rival network. He needed to make a decision. What could Cole do for him? He needed to know *now*. Cole dragged a hand over his damp brow. This deal was major, major. If this didn't happen, Hunter Broadcasting was in deep trouble.

Feeling that cold sweat break behind his neck now, Cole stabbed a few keys. He was talking, trying to mend a critical situation, when Taryn wandered back and peered in at him, questioning, through the window. Needing to talk to Liam— with no distractions—Cole angled away.

Even as they spoke, Cole's brain was shouting at him. *Why*

did you let down your guard? If he cruised for long enough, of course something bad would happen. And as the negotiations deteriorated, and Taryn, worried and disappointed, moved inside her house, Cole made a vow. If only this worked out, if he didn't lose this deal and have to put off workers, need to shut down shows, he would never take his position for granted again.

Not for any reason.

Not for anyone.

"I'm ba-ack!"

With his usual cheery smile, Roman Lyons moved into Taryn's office at Hunter Broadcasting and, at her desk, set a big "friends only" kiss upon her cheek.

Genuinely happy to see him, trying to tack up a smile, Taryn set down her pen. "How was the script-writing junket?"

"Junket?" Roman swung a leg over the corner of her desk. "I'll have you know that my colleagues and I worked bloody hard on sorting out angles and zingers for our next and biggest season yet. Did you miss me?"

"Terribly."

"Good job I was only gone a week then." Roman leaned closer. "So, tell me. Has the Commander finally given your show the nod? You've been back from that survey two weeks. The budget's been worked over a thousand times. Surely he's made a decision."

When her insides ached, she could only look away.

While they hadn't discussed it, Taryn guessed Roman knew she and Cole were lovers. Or *had* been. Frankly, she was confused at how things had turned out, although she guessed she shouldn't be surprised. Since that Friday, just over a week ago, when Cole had needed to perform circus tricks to keep that football contract from going down in a landslide, things had changed between them. For the worse.

Although they saw each other at work and a couple of times had gone out to lunch, Cole had distanced himself. He hadn't come over to her place, hadn't invited her to his. Whenever she suggested they do something fun, he said he was far too busy. If she brought up her show, he told her he'd get back to her soon.

Of course, Cole blamed himself for the panic that had ensued when that man, Liam Finlay, had been unable to get in contact the afternoon they'd played hooky in the park. And, although he would never admit it, or accuse her, she was certain Cole blamed her, too, for tempting him outside of his usual dutiful boundaries.

She'd never been a party girl, but that week with Cole had been the best of her life. More than that, she'd reevaluated. Thought about priorities. She still wanted her show to go into production, but she'd come to see that in recent years she hadn't laughed enough. She'd usually taken herself so seriously. Last week, Vi had said she was a different woman. Hell, Taryn had thought Cole had become a different man.

Apparently not.

Taryn answered Roman's question. "Cole put through word today. *Hot Spots* has his approval."

Roman's expression exploded. Giving a hoot, he swung an arm through the air.

"That, my lovely, deserves a celebration. Cups of tea all around." Jumping off the desk, he eyed her percolator. "Although coffee will more than suffice."

The news had come via email and was signed, Best, Cole Hunter, Executive Producer In Charge. Certainly everyone had a template, but couldn't he have given her this news in person?

While Roman moved over to that counter, Taryn sucked down a fortifying breath. She didn't have to confess anything to this man. Except, firstly she trusted him. And secondly she'd felt so isolated, so alone here since Cole had bit by bit shut her out. She needed catharsis. To purge her doubts. Clear her conscience.

"I suppose you figured it out," she began.

Roman was lumping sugar into his cup. "Figured out what?"

"That we…that Cole and I have been, well, *together*."

Roman hesitated only a second before pouring the coffee. "Totally your business."

"I didn't do it to gain the advantage," she said. "I didn't sell myself to get my show through. It happened and now *Hot Spots* will go into production…"

Roman returned with two cups. "And that is top news."

She shut her eyes but those doubts wouldn't leave her. "I can't stop wondering if Cole finally slid it through because he felt obligated. He never approved of the idea. He never stopped telling me he thought it would fail."

"Here's a big tip." Roman pulled in a chair. "Don't torture yourself. Just run with it and give those ratings a jolly good jolt."

She half smiled but had to ask. "Has this ever happened before? Cole getting involved with a colleague, I mean."

"Cole's not the blast-his-own-horn kind of guy. Or, rather, not with regard to love affairs. Low-key. As far as I know, no one from here. And never anything serious."

"Guess that hasn't changed."

Roman heaved out a breath and gave her a comforting smile. "It's not your fault. You know what they say about a leopard and his spots."

Around ten, Roman said *cheerio*. At the exact moment he left, Cole strode by her office without slowing down.

A hollow gutted feeling gripped her and wouldn't let go. The walls seemed to fade back at the same time they pressed in. She set her face in her palms and tried to fathom this out.

From the moment they'd first kissed, she'd known what she was getting into. Trouble. But there'd been a time when she'd thought she'd meant something more than a convenience to him. Another element in his world to be manipulated. Eliminated.

Seems she'd been wrong.

An urge overwhelmed her. An impulse greater than she'd ever known. Taryn pushed back her chair and, needing answers or closure or *something,* she caught up with him outside of the accounts department. Cole obviously hadn't thought she'd put on a chase. He jumped when he saw her appear beside him.

A little out of breath, she asked, "Any more word?"

His Adam's apple bobbed above his tie's Windsor knot then control returned to his face.

"Word on what?"

"Your father's situation."

"No breakthroughs yet although I have every confidence Brandon will come through. If you'll excuse me, I have a meeting. I'm already late."

He headed off, but she wasn't finished.

"Still thinking about sending Tate to your brother's?" she asked, catching up again.

"That's one plan."

Not willing to talk about it? *Okay. Next.*

"I finally got Muffin inside. She's had her kittens. Four in all."

"I hope they find good homes."

Still walking, she said, "I thought you might want to see the rundown for the first show. It's in draft form—"

"Leave it with my PA. You know Leslie."

His personal assistant was a nice lady with the patience of a saint. She'd need to be, working with Cole.

"Any special requests to be included in the draft?"

"Just slot out your expanded ideas for the six locations—"

She didn't hear the rest. She slapped a hand on his arm to try to pull him up.

"What do you mean *six*? A season is thirteen episodes."

"We'll see about that after initial ratings come in."

"I'm not happy with six shows, Cole. You're not giving it a chance."

He was checking his watch, edging away up the hall. "Like I said…"

She growled. If he said just one more time he was late…

She blurted it out. "Why are you treating me like this?"

Darren from the Sport department was walking by, slowing down to take a good long look. Cole took her arm and led her into a nearby unused office.

After shutting the door, he set his hands low on his hips. "You want to cause a scene?"

"I want some answers."

"Six shows is my limit, Taryn." His chin notched up. "I don't recall promising you anything."

So she should be grateful?

"I don't recall asking for anything other than you meeting the terms of my contract."

He folded his arms, cocked his head. "Are you done?"

"No. I'm not done. I want to say you don't have to go around hiding from me anymore."

"I don't hide from anyone."

"If you regret that time away, that week when we came back and were happy, it's not half as much as I do."

She'd said the words. How much easier her life would be if she believed them.

"You're jumping to conclusions," he said.

"I'm inventing the fact that you're avoiding me?"

His eyes slowly narrowed.

"Do you want to know how I've been filling in my time

these past days? Not only have I got that murder mystery hanging over my head, my brother Dex has managed to get himself tangled up in some blackmail scheme."

"Since when?"

"Dex mentioned it last night when he called. He clammed up when I asked questions. But that's not enough. He's kindly informed me that the finances over there are dangling by a bare-assed thread."

"He actually said that?"

Cole's jaw shifted. "Well, no. Not in so many words. But I can hear in his voice that he's worried." His chin went up. "Add to that the fact Liam Finlay informed me that he's still an inch away from accepting another network's deal. That's where I'm headed now, if you care to know. To try to avoid that last looming disaster from falling on our heads."

Not only were his irises dangerously dark, the half-moons underneath his eyes were dark, too. Not nearly enough sleep. Taryn knew what that was like. But she didn't have the weight of the future of at least two multimillion-dollar enterprises riding on her back. She was simply trying to survive an ill-fated love affair. Get her show the time on air she believed it deserved.

"I didn't know," she muttered. "You didn't say."

His tone dropped. "I could have come to you and whined and moaned, but that's not what I do. I fix things. I take responsibility."

All the emotions she carried around trapped deep inside of her these past days began to bubble up and spill over. If he'd made her feel insignificant before, now she felt as inconsequential as a gnat. Her gaze dropped to her shoes. Her vision blurred. God, she wanted to die.

She heard him exhale and a moment later two fingers were under her chin, lifting her face until, her throat thick, she was peering into his eyes.

"I'm sorry I haven't had two minutes to spare lately," he said. "That doesn't mean I didn't enjoy our time together. But pizza and rerelease DVDs are out of the question right now." His fingers slid down her arm until he was holding her hand. "You understand, don't you?"

Taryn sagged into herself. She'd started out wanting to corner him and yet she'd been the one who was crowded back and bombarded until her head was left spinning. But at least now she had an explanation for his lack of interest. If she looked at it logically rather than emotionally, he had a good reason. She supposed.

She found the wherewithal to nod.

"I guess I understand."

"Will you be all right getting back to your office?" She nodded again. "Okay." He pressed a lingering kiss on her cheek. "I really have to go."

He strode away, leaving her alone, numb, and the door wide-open for everyone to see.

Seventeen

Taryn usually enjoyed seeing her aunt. But tonight's visit she could have done without. Not because Vi had done anything disagreeable. They hadn't had an argument since high school when Taryn had decided she had more important things to do than keep her room halfway clean and suffer regular homework.

But when Vi had rung and invited herself over for dinner, Taryn wanted to postpone. She wouldn't make good company. She only wanted to sit around alone and keep rehashing in her mind whether or not she ought to have forgiven Cole for his recent behavior.

Her stronger self wanted to tell him to take a hike. Who needed to feel like a convenience? She also wanted to give Cole the benefit of the doubt. Maybe when this particularly tough time in his life was over, he would miraculously revert to the charming, at times sensitive man she'd discovered on that island.

Passion. Desire. A constant need to be close. Until now she'd never been able to comprehend how a woman could get so caught up in those kinds of emotions that she could act in ways that would normally make her retch. She understood better now. It was as if she were *infected* by him. Her blood, her heart, her mind.

When she'd confronted him yesterday, she'd held out hope that he would at least make a small effort and drop by her office today. He hadn't. And tomorrow…? Hell, he had to talk to her *sometime*. They worked together, for Pete's sake.

As Taryn sat with her aunt in her living room, with Vi nattering on about how gorgeous the new kittens were, she realized her aunt had asked a question. Realigning her thoughts, Taryn smiled over.

"Sorry. What was that?"

"I was asking if that man at your work had gotten any closer to letting you know whether your show will go ahead."

"He made his decision yesterday. We start production next week."

Vi jumped in her seat then grabbed her niece to give her a big hug.

"I'm so proud of you. Not that I ever had a doubt. That other lot was mad to let you go. But, see, it's all worked out for the best. You're with a company who respect who you are and what you can give." Reaching down, Vi preened Muffin's head where the mother cat lay in her big open box by their feet. "I must say, I was beginning to wonder when your boss would get around to making it official. It's been over two weeks since you got back from that survey. Was he very difficult while you were away? You'd told me he was a bit of a tyrant at the office."

"We…came to an understanding."

Vi stopped stroking and tilted her head. "An understanding, darling?"

"Or I thought we had."

"I'm not sure I understand."

"I'm not sure I understand, either."

Vi's voice and shoulders dropped. "He took advantage of you, didn't he?"

As that sick ache spread in her chest, Taryn shut her eyes. She could say that she had no idea what her aunt was talking about. She could tell Vi that she wasn't in high school anymore. She didn't have to clean her room if she didn't want to, and she could sleep with a man—this man—if she chose. But Vi wasn't attacking her. Her aunt loved her, had always taken care of her and never failed to give the best advice.

"He didn't take advantage of me," Taryn finally said. "I wanted it to happen. He's an extremely charismatic man."

Vi's brows sloped as if she'd figured that out.

"From the moment we met," Taryn went on, "there's been a thing between us. You know. A connection."

"An attraction."

"It would have happened eventually whether we went away together or not."

"So you don't regret it?"

"I didn't *think* I would."

Taryn explained about the attempt on Guthrie Hunter's life. She told Vi how much Cole seemed to have appreciated her support when they'd called into the Hunter home that night. She also told her about all the trouble at Hunters in L.A. and of Cole's concerns regarding that big sporting contract.

While she talked on, Vi listened, nodding at certain points, scowling when it was appropriate. Taryn ended by saying that over the past week, Cole's affections and attention toward her had cooled. Actually, other than that token brush of his lips over her cheek yesterday before leaving her alone in that empty office, his dealings with her verged on chilly.

"But when he explained what was behind his being so distant, I understood. Or I tried to." When her aunt remained quiet, Taryn asked, "Don't you have any advice?"

"I'm not sure you want to hear it."

"Other than suggesting I should lower my hem or not leave assignments till the last minute, I can't remember a time I didn't take your advice."

Vi's attention dropped again to Muffin and her week-old litter of three.

"You'd spoken about this cat for months," she said. "How you'd call to her, lay food trails for her, how you'd even tried to pounce on her a couple of times. You figured that once you got her inside, she'd want to stay."

Taryn wasn't certain where this was headed. "She looks happy enough now she's here."

"Do you think she would have been if you'd caught her and locked her up in this house?"

Taryn blinked. "I was trying to help."

"You wanted to give her a home here with you. But if you'd forced her, chances are she'd only want to escape."

"You're saying I should let Cole do what he wants—let him go—and maybe, one day, he'll come back to me." Taryn shrank back. "I can't do that."

"You can't force someone to act a certain way, either."

"Like be halfway decent?"

Why should Cole have it all his way? By nature, she was a reserved person who tolerated much, but she did not like to be used—taken for granted—and Vi's advice seemed to insinuate that she do and accept just that.

Vi stood. "I'll get dinner on. I brought blueberry pastries for a treat afterward."

Vi was heading toward the kitchen when Taryn said, "I remember when I was very young, you dated a man. He was nice from what I recall. You were happy. But one night I heard a disagreement and we never saw him again."

Vi nodded as if she remembered it well. "That was a long time ago."

"I'd hoped that you two would get married," Taryn confessed.

"I'd hoped for that, too. Marty was a wonderful man, married before with three children all around your age."

"What went wrong, Vi? What was the argument about?"

"Marty was a family man. He would've liked nothing more than to have made his family with us."

"And he loved you."

"I believe he did. I most certainly loved him."

Taryn held her swooping stomach. "It wasn't because of me, was it? The reason you broke up."

Vi laughed and crossed back over. "You were an angel. Still are. Marty said often what a good girl you were. That you and I were lucky to have each other. It tore him up that he could only see his own children every other weekend."

"So his wife hadn't passed away."

"They were divorced. He said it was the hardest thing in the world to pack his bags and know that from that moment on his family would be forever fractured. We'd been seeing each other for six months when he asked his children if they'd like to meet a special lady and her niece. They'd innocently told their mother. Suddenly she wanted him back."

"So no one else could have him."

"He didn't contact me for a few days after that. Then, that night you remember, he tried to explain how cornered he felt. I didn't understand. Or didn't want to. If he loved me, he wouldn't consider going back to live with another woman, even the mother of his children." Vi's eyes began to glisten. "I couldn't bear the thought of his sleeping in the same bed with her, of her kissing him good-night when I was the one who loved him, not her."

Feeling sick for her all these years later, Taryn reached up to hold her aunt's hands. "But you said you'd wait for him, right?"

"I told him that if he was even considering that, he could go now. Or he could do the decent thing and tell me, then and there, that he was staying where he was, with us." She sighed. "He left. I was so upset. As far as I could see, he mustn't have loved me. Or, at least, not enough."

"Maybe you did the right thing."

Vi's resigned look returned. "Three months later, his ex kicked him out again. I saw his photo in the back pages of a paper three years later. He'd married a woman with a big bright smile. I wondered if they'd be happy together. I wondered if she loved him as much as I still did."

Taryn slowly got to her feet. "I never knew."

Never had any idea. Vi was a person who rolled up her sleeves and got on with things. But she was also a woman, with emotions, passions, like everyone else.

When her aunt inhaled deeply, Taryn knew she was willing back tears.

"So, you see," Vi said, "you can't force someone to stay. You have to let them make up their own mind. And there are no rules to say that decisions that might seem easy for one aren't incredibly difficult for another. When I look back now, if I'd been him, I would have gone back to her, too."

Taryn thought about that, but it was obvious. "Because of the children."

Muffin let out a loud *meow* and Vi brought herself back. "I think she's telling us dinner is long overdue."

Wanting to cry for her, Taryn wrapped her arms around her aunt. "I'm so glad you came today. So thankful you've always been there for me."

Vi hugged her back, stroked her hair. "I wouldn't have had it any other way."

Cole glanced at the time on his laptop screen then rubbed a hand over his stinging eyes. He was beat. Time to knock off.

Time he ate. But he still had so much to do trying to figure out how to shuffle the figures in L.A. so Hunter Productions could enter the next season as strongly as possible.

What he'd much rather do is drop by Taryn's place and take her out to dinner. Only, like the rest of the East Coast, given the time, she would already have eaten. And, besides, he wasn't good for her right now. Or was that she wasn't good for him? Either way, a man could only have one mistress, and his was Hunter Enterprises. He couldn't let the company—his family and mother's memory—down again. Not for a woman. Even a woman like Taryn.

His cell phone buzzed. Cole read the ID. A rush of heat filled his neck, his head, his chest. Two deep breaths and he connected. His brother's smooth baritone echoed down the line.

"Hope I didn't wake you," Dex said.

"I don't get the luxury of much sleep these days."

"In a happy mood as usual, I see."

Cole bit down. What must it be like to go through life pretending you had nothing more to worry about than which starlet you were going to sleep with next?

He ground out, "What do you want?"

"To brighten your day. The revenue figures are in on our latest release. After a huge opening weekend, we're solid, sitting well on top of the black."

Cole let the line hang.

"Cole, you there?"

"Uh-huh."

"Aren't you even slightly pleased?"

"I'm waiting."

"What for?"

"The bad news."

Dex laughed, a deep and carefree sound. He'd been the same since they were kids. Dex was the charmer, who managed to wiggle in and out of trouble without getting so much as a scratch, while Cole was busy learning the business, making sure someone of integrity would one day take over what their grandfather and father had worked so hard to build. Dex didn't seem to worry too much about any of that.

Eyeing Brandon and Jeremy Judge's latest report lying read twice on his desk, Cole asked, "Want the latest on Dad?"

"What's happening there? Tate all right now?"

"He's fine."

Cole gave a rundown on security measures and the fact Brandon was working hard with Judge to uncover new leads.

Dex got back to Tate. "Well, if the little guy wants to come over for a visit…"

"That's funny. Take a five-year-old away from kidnapping troubles to put him with a man who is the target of a blackmail campaign."

"I told you not to worry about that." Dex grunted. "I must have been raving mad letting that slip in the first place."

"If I don't worry, who will?"

Dex pushed out a breath. "All I'm saying is that Tate is welcome anytime."

"Who have you got lined up to babysit? Some Hollywood starlet you're screwing?"

The line went deathly quiet. "Be careful, bro. You might find reward in your near monklike lifestyle, the fact you get off on telling everyone how hard you work and how no one appreciates what you do, but I intend to go on enjoying what a man is meant to enjoy."

"That would be an endless string of empty affairs."

"You're a sanctimonious son of a—"

The conversation went downhill from there.

Cole was still fuming when he left the building an hour later. How could two brothers be so different? Birth order? A swap at the hospital the day Dex was born? Although, Cole

could admit, Dex had got the tail end of his latest foul mood.
At least that new release was doing well. There was still the
problem of Tate. Hopefully his little brother wouldn't be involved in any future incidents, but should Tate happen to get
hurt in any way because of this murder attempt mess, Cole
would feel directly responsible. He didn't want Tate to get
mixed up in Dex's blackmail business, if it came to anything.
Then again, what could be worse than living with Eloise as a
mother? The answer was the possibility of being shoved in a
van never to be seen or heard from again.

Cole was driving on autopilot when he noticed the sign
announcing the arterial route to Taryn's neighborhood. She
might think he hadn't thought much about her lately. Truth
was he'd thought about her a great deal. Way too much. Another reason he wasn't getting much sleep.

This past week he'd had to put up a barrier between them.
Not that he'd wanted to, but, frankly, she'd been interfering
with his responsibilities. And, to be fair, he'd let himself get
sidetracked. Taryn's company was always preferable to flog-
ging himself with budget and technical reports, proposals
and financial crises. But if *he* didn't cover all the bases, who
would? Admittedly, Roman Lyons was proving to be a big
ongoing help. His father, however, barely came into the office anymore, which, Cole supposed, meant less likelihood
of decisions needing to be reversed.

That brought him back to Taryn.

He couldn't risk distractions. While she was employed by
Hunter Broadcasting, he would know little relief. He'd okayed
her show out of obligation more than anything. A sense of
loyalty, or maybe expectation. And while that may be under-
standable, given the nature of the time they'd spent together,
he wasn't looking forward to the anticipated hit to the company. Hell, he'd just chastised Dex for not thinking with his
head. Recently, had he been any better?

Setting his jaw, Cole stepped on the gas and drove past that turnoff.

Grandpa Hunter used to say, *There's no better time for change than the present.*

No smarter time than now to move on.

Eighteen

Taryn took her aunt's advice. She would never again consider hounding Cole, like she had that day a week ago when he'd informed her that her show would record six episodes rather than a full season's complement of thirteen. Now she didn't seek out his company and most certainly he didn't seek out hers.

As the days had gone by, she'd kept herself busy with one of two occupations. She was either immersed in her show's preparation—organizing crew, sponsors, studio time—or sourcing people who would love to adopt a kitten.

She did little socially, although when Roman had asked, she'd gone to a movie. They'd grabbed a bite beforehand, had enjoyed buttered popcorn throughout the show and had said goodbye in the complex's parking lot.

Given he knew about the Cole situation, Taryn guessed Roman felt sorry for her. Which was thoughtful. Nice. But she was done with feeling sorry for herself.

Over the past couple of days, her hope to stay with Hunter Broadcasting had dimmed. She'd swallowed the six-show deal. But then Cole had cut her budget in half. Had told her that he could not agree to sign the host she liked. Today he'd put the nail in her coffin. His PA had passed on the news that rather than five people helping to put the show together, she'd have two, one being a seventeen-year-old graduate. No experience equaled cheap labor.

Technically, Cole might have approved her show but, clearly, he still wanted her gone. She hoped he slept well at night.

Earlier today, Taryn had learned Guthrie was in, which happened less and less. When Taryn had phoned through, his personal assistant had said he'd see her straightaway.

Walking down that long corridor, Taryn guessed she ought to feel nervous, one of the reasons being that she didn't normally do snap decisions. Usually she formulated a plan, studied all the angles then pursued her goal until said goal was attained. Whereas the action she'd decided upon this morning had seemed to come to her out of the blue. Kind of the way she'd handled her conflagration of an affair with Cole. Only, no matter how much this might hurt, she was certain this decision was the right one.

She entered Guthrie's office. He stood by that long stretch of window, studying that panoramic view of Sydney and its harbor, his fingers loosely thatched at his back. Hearing her, he turned, smiled and asked, "What can I do for you, Taryn?"

They took seats and suddenly Taryn couldn't find the right words. While the son might be difficult, Guthrie had only ever been supportive. But, whether he knew it or not, Guthrie wasn't in charge here. If he were, she wouldn't need to jump through Cole's endless hoops.

Taryn looked Guthrie in the eye. "I have to leave Hunter Broadcasting."

His eyebrows snapped together. "Trouble with staff?"

"With management." She swallowed. "With Cole."

Guthrie studied her for a long queasy moment. Then he pushed to his feet and, with a slight limp leftover from that last assault, crossed to his desk.

"I'll have a word with him," he said, stabbing a button. "Stay put. We'll sort this out."

"That won't do any good." Having found her feet, too, she moved closer.

Guthrie had the receiver to his ear. "He has his own mind, but Cole listens when he knows I'm serious."

She was serious, too. "He doesn't believe in my project. I won't put my all into doing my best when Cole is doing everything in his power to cut me off at the knees."

Guthrie tried again. "My son's motives can seem harsh at times, but underneath all the woo-hah, he's only trying to take care of things."

"I believe you. I do. But it doesn't work in this situation." *Doesn't work for me.*

"Taryn, are you certain there's nothing more behind this? I was preoccupied that afternoon you both flew back from that survey, but…"

"Whatever happened between the two of us doesn't change his work attitude, then or now. I'm unhappy here." Not appreciated or respected. Cole had seduced her and, yes, she'd wanted to be seduced. He liked to be in charge, but in this final stretch, she was taking the reins.

"I wish it were different," she said, "but I don't ever see that changing. I'll leave Hunters today."

Despite today's heavy rain, Taryn had ventured out to collect some cat milk for Muffin and a bunch of roses from the corner store. She was arranging the flowers in her favorite vase, thinking about dicing some vitamin-rich food for the lactating mother, when a knock sounded on the door. She glanced up. She wasn't expecting her aunt. Her friends all had jobs during the week. Perhaps it was a delivery, only she wasn't expecting an order.

As she passed by Muffin and her litter, who were snuggled

and asleep in a large bed-box in the living room, Taryn had a flash but quickly pushed the thought aside. Guthrie had accepted her resignation and she didn't regret the move. The CEO slash Executive Producer of Hunter Broadcasting had never liked her show's premise. Had never approved of her being hired without being consulted first. No doubt, when all was said and done, Cole would be grateful to be rid of that headache. She was relieved to have gotten rid of hers. She was more calm. Her usual cool self again.

Then Taryn fanned back the door and her heart leaped so high, she had to swallow to push the lump halfway back down. Cole stood on her porch, looking unhappy about being drenched because of the rain and, she supposed, being here. Well, he could simply turn around, jump in his sports car and go back to the office. She certainly hadn't invited him.

Cole set his monster black umbrella down, tapping the steel spike against the timber floorboards twice—to help shake off the water or make certain she was paying attention?

"What's this about you quitting?"

She feigned surprise. "You're only finding out now? I gave Guthrie my resignation two days ago."

"Did you think to consult me?"

"Consider yourself consulted." Her hand still on the doorknob, she stepped back. "Hope I don't sound rude, but I was in the middle of something important."

"Finding another job?"

"Feeding the cat."

Her face and neck hot, she moved to shut the door. One big black leather lace-up slid out, acting as a stop.

He said, "You don't have to leave."

"It was a choice, Cole. I don't have to go. I *want* to go." She slanted her head. "Why are you here? You never liked my idea. You've done everything you could to have me land flat on my backside." *You've ignored me day after day.*

"I'll come in and we'll discuss it."

"I'm not letting you in." Not ever again. "Give yourself until next week. You'll have forgotten all about this by then."

Setting his umbrella up against the outside wall, he dragged a hand down his face as if this were all too hard.

"Look, I'm sorry I had to make all those cuts."

"That's fine. All forgotten. Now please leave."

He cast an exasperated look back at the rain teeming down beyond her porch and exhaled.

"I can't help the way things are," he said. "You knew what my life was from the start."

When heat from frustration and anger threatened to overtake her, she closed her eyes and shook her head. If he felt guilty about the way he'd treated her, that was his bad luck. She only wanted him to vanish so she could go back to arranging flowers and forgetting that man ever existed.

"Let me in. We'll talk—"

As he moved forward, finished with games, she moved, too. And shut the door.

But Cole's barrier now was a thousand times more effective than the one he'd used earlier. He reached out and, without apology, hooked one arm around her waist then hauled her close until her breasts were pressed against his shirt and she felt the booming of his heartbeat too near her own.

She opened her mouth to tear him down. After what he'd done, how dare he handle her this way. But in one blinding heartbeat, his mouth had taken hers. With one palm supporting the small of her back, he kissed her long and hard and shockingly deep. Flames swirled through her blood, instantly melting her bones, causing her to become a rag doll in his arms.

But when his palm scooped lower and she felt him harden against her belly, her strength returned. Making fists, she pushed with both barrels against his chest. She might as well have tried to shift a mountain. He was on a mission. And, damn the man, he was winning.

As his head angled more and the rough of his beard rubbed a path against her cheek, gradually, bit by bit, her fight drained away. He was so determined, so *hot,* what hope did she have? But she wasn't beaten so much as temporarily tamed. If he'd only quit with the caveman act—if he'd stop kissing her long enough for her to get her thoughts together—she'd tell him this kind of treatment wouldn't change her mind...

never...

ever.

By the time his mouth eventually left hers, the world was spinning twice as fast. Not only were her breasts aching, begging for his touch, the throbbing at the apex of her thighs told her that past indiscretions were forgiven. Forgotten.

As his lidded eyes searched hers, Taryn couldn't bring herself to move away. She could only remember the heaven she'd experienced on that island when he'd coaxed and adored her body, teasing her nipples, stroking her curves, loving her to the point where nothing and no one else had existed.

Then, over the pounding rain, she heard another noise. His cell phone sounding. Rather than take the call, he pressed soft moist kisses at one corner of her mouth while two hot fingers rode a drugging circle low on her back. But his cell beeped again, and again. Giddy with want, she felt his hesitation and forced herself to focus. The sound of the rain drifted back in. Behind her, Muffin mewed twice. When Cole carefully released her, the firm set of his jaw said he wasn't finished sorting this out but he also needed to read that text.

Crawling out from the fog, Taryn remembered Aunt Vi's advice. Keep the door open because once it's shut, there's no going back. But when Cole held up one finger to ask her to hold on a minute, Taryn touched her still-burning lips and a good measure of the stardust faded and fell away. She watched him check the cell, dial into his voice mail, then press a finger to an ear, shutting out a roll of thunder while he turned his back to concentrate fully on business.

Taryn blinked and thought, but when she'd made up her mind, she didn't bother to interrupt. She simply shut the door, bolted the lock and didn't open it again, no matter how hard he knocked.

With two chilled beers in hand, Cole sidled up to the chair next to Brandon's. Talking above the din of the local club, he handed one over and asked, "So, anything to report?"

"Judge and I have exhausted every lead from the guy who threw himself under that car. If he was connected to those earlier incidents and this latest one, whoever's pulling the strings has done a fine job of camouflaging their trail. I've assigned a private detail for Guthrie's and Tate's protection. I also suggested one for your stepmother, but she declined."

Cole nodded then downed a mouthful of beer.

Brandon went on to describe in detail the areas he would sweep next: again questioning neighbors and also employees, setting up surveillance cameras that reached outside of normal parameters. Cole absorbed it all at the same time as his brain switched to a different box in his head. Lately, more and more, he found his thoughts drifting there and wanting to stay.

He thought he knew himself pretty well and yet he was stumped figuring out why he'd bothered showing up on Taryn's doorstep the other day. She was right. Although he'd enjoyed their time together, he'd never gone for her show's concept. Obligation had caused him to okay it. Duty had compelled him to sabotage it. Guilt had sent him knocking on her door to… Apologize? Make amends?

Hell, he was a fool and he knew it.

"Any questions?"

Cole blinked back. "About what?"

"You didn't hear anything I just said, did you?"

"Of course I did. This is my father's life we're talking about."

"Which means whatever it is eating you must be important."

Cole swirled his bottle. No reason he couldn't share with his best friend. If anyone would understand, it was Brandon.

"It's a woman. Taryn Quinn."

Brandon sat slowly back. "You blew it?"

"I let it go."

He explained the story from go to woe.

"Holy crap," Brandon said when Cole had finished. "No wonder she's pissed at you. You sleep with her like there's no tomorrow then barely acknowledge her because of a contract. To add insult to injury, you set her show up for a slide into the mud."

Cole cocked an eyebrow, swallowed beer. "That's pretty much it."

"You might be company obsessed, but you've never treated a woman like that before."

Gazing at his beer, Cole confessed, "Taryn's special."

"God help the ones who aren't."

"I have too much on my plate, too much to keep in order, to have to worry about a relationship."

"Like Meredith said at the reunion, you can't run forever."

"I can try."

"You need to ease up on yourself. Quit taking all the responsibility for Hunters. That's too much for anyone."

"You say that as if I have a choice."

"Oh, it's a choice, all right. Don't try to say you don't *like* being 'the man.' At school, if you didn't get 'school captain this' or 'regional champion that,' you dragged your feet for days."

"It's healthy to be competitive. It's natural."

"Until it starts to screw with your life."

"Work *is* my life. With all my family tangled up in it, it has to be."

"I'll give you my take. I think this woman's in love with you. And my bet is you're in love with her, too."

After the moment of shock had passed, Cole barked out a laugh. "Remember who you're talking to? I've *never* been in love." He held up a warning finger. "Meredith McReedy doesn't count. Hell, I've only known Taryn a few weeks."

"Sometimes it happens that way. Fast and deadly, like a snake bite."

"I'm not looking to get hitched."

"All I've heard about this lady is how strong and beautiful and perfect she is. But you're not really seeing it."

Cole drained the rest of his beer then set the bottle down on the table hard. "I don't see any ring on your fat finger."

"Maybe that's because I haven't found the right person."

Cole's thoughts skidded to a halt as those words echoed through his brain.

Was that it? Why he couldn't for the life of him shake her from his mind. And the fascination was growing worse every day. Love? It was great his mother and father had shared it. He'd always thought that *someday* he'd settle down, too.

Question was, if Brandon was right—if this was it and she was the one—given that she hated his guts...

What did he do now?

The next day was Saturday. At home, Cole was about to settle down with that pain-in-the-butt Liam Finlay contract yet again. He got this was an important deal with a *huge* amount of money hanging in the balance, but he was beginning to wonder if Finlay was playing games, stretching this out, making him suffer because of his past unsatisfactory dealings with Guthrie. Still, what could he do? Hunter Broad-

casting needed this deal. Therefore Cole couldn't slack off.
Or, rather, not again.

His home phone extension rang. Business calls came
through on his cell. Majority of his personal calls, too. Probably some poor sales sap doing another cold call. Or…

Tate knew that number. He'd learned it off by heart. When
the phone stopped then rang again, a shiver ran through Cole's
blood and he picked up. Sure enough, that familiar sweet voice
filtered down the line.

"Daddy's not home and Mommy says I'm too noisy," Tate
said. "She's tired."

"Where your dad?"

It was the weekend and Guthrie had been spending most
of his time at home lately. Where else might he be?

"Don't know." Cole imagined Tate's little shoulders shrugging. "Can you come and play with me?"

Cole recalled that tome of a contract sitting on his home
desk. There was loads of other work he could catch up on,
too. But then he thought of Tate, what a bum deal he'd gotten having a mother like Eloise, feeling as if he had to get
around like a mouse when he was a robust five-year-old boy
who should be out kicking a ball, not stuck inside playing
with electronic games.

Cole scrubbed his jaw, made his decision.

"Are you watching TV, kiddo?"

"Uh-huh. *SpongeBob*'s just started." Tate laughed. "He's
funny."

"Grab a hat. By the time your show's over, I'll be there."

Cole arrived bang on time and let Creepy Nancy know that
he was taking Tate out for the day. Eloise didn't bother to come
downstairs to say have a nice time. Wearing a bright red tee,
Tate sat like an angel in the passenger-side seat while they
drove to a park, the one Cole and Taryn had paddled those

boats in, not that he'd intentionally planned his and Tate's time together today that way.

Cole parked and grabbed the football he'd brought along. They filled their stomachs with hot dogs and Coke first. Watched the ducks on the lake while the food settled. When Cole couldn't control Tate's fidgets any longer, they kicked and tossed the pigskin back and forth. Cole showed his brother techniques required for a handball, a pass famous in Aussie Rules Football. Tate was doing well, stepping into the action, getting his punching fist almost right. They'd been out an hour. Given Tate wasn't nearly tired yet, Cole was thinking about teaching him a torpedo punt kick when his cell phone buzzed.

"This might be your dad," he called out to Tate, who was perhaps twenty yards away. But when Cole answered without checking the ID, the voice on the other end wasn't the one he'd expected.

"Liam Finlay here."

Cole's every sense zoomed in to concentrate fully on this conversation. "What's up?"

"My lawyers are with me. There's another conflict, page 103, item 24."

Cole's mind flew back, trying to identify the passage.

Liam went on to inform him that now the Players Association weren't happy with their cut, given the exclusivity clause relating to live games televised. Cole replied they'd been through this just last week. He'd already bumped his offer up. Liam said the dotted line was still blank. Now was the time to iron these creases out. Cole said he didn't want to increase his offer. He didn't believe anyone would. Liam said that was up to him. He could give him an answer now or come to the headquarters and talk it through.

A red soccer ball shot up and hit Cole in the shin, on the same leg that bore that old cubby house scar. In that instant, Cole remembered his brothers, Dex, Wynn, Tate—

His head snapped up. He looked left, right. Then the panic, cold and creeping, began to seep into his bones.

Cole spun a three-sixty. Looked down low. Up high. Behind benches and trees. His world shrank then funneled out fast. That tiny five-year-old was nowhere to be seen.

He held his stomach as it pitched and pitched again. He didn't often pray but now he looked to heaven and, as the strength seemed to drain from his body and his brain began to tingle, he vowed he would give anything—*everything*—if he was only overreacting and Tate would magically reappear.

On the ground, a toss away, Cole spotted his cell. His scattered thoughts pieced together. If Tate was indeed missing—and given recent history, that idea couldn't be discounted—there was a logical step he must take. Sending another swift glance around, he scooped up the phone where he'd dropped it then frowned at the noise coming out. Finlay was still bleating on the other end?

Cole didn't think twice.

He ended that call.

While he strode around, asking the ice-cream vendor then a man walking his dog if they'd seen a little boy in a bright red tee, he dialed the three-digit number to connect to emergency services. As he spoke to the representative on the other end of the line, sickening panic crushed in again, but this time it was peppered with resolve. If Tate was lost, if he'd been taken, he *would* find his brother. If he had to ask every person in this park, cut down every tree, check on each—

Cole's tracking gaze stopped and he froze.

In the parking lot some fifty yards away, a big black van was reversing out. The windows tinted an impenetrable shade, Cole couldn't make out the plates but, through the windshield, he saw the shaggy-haired driver wore dark glasses that covered half his face. His father had said one of the men who'd tried to abduct Tate had shaggy hair, big black glasses. Cole also knew those men had driven a black van.

Cole belted off. He heard Tate's name called out. Twice. Three times. Limbs pumping, he realized that voice was his own.

He slammed into the van before it could leave, thumped on the sliding door and didn't stop. The driver, an angry weedy man, soon appeared.

"What the hell you doing to my vehicle?"

Cole grabbed him by the scruff of his shirt and pulled him up so he could talk to his weasel face. "Open that door. Do it now. *Now!*"

If he was right, if Tate was in there, he'd deal with weasel-man after his brother was out in the light again. But when he flung aside the door, peered inside, the space was empty other than an old washing machine dumped in one corner.

Cole stormed over, his footfalls echoing through the metal cage. He flung open the lid of the machine and then—

His heart dropped to the ground. He staggered back.

Empty.

Cole wandered out into the sunshine feeling sucker punched. He was the son who always had things under control. He couldn't stand to have surprises sneak up and bite him in the rear. He complained about Dex, about Wynn. Huffed at memories of a grown woman like Teagan having her own life. He'd thought he was so much better, responsible, worthier than any of them.

And here he'd failed in the most devastating way possible. How would he ever tell his father?

People were milling around him. Cole knew he must look like a madman. On a different level, he understood he needed to get himself together. He couldn't help Tate if he disintegrated into a mute, dazed mess.

Cole cast another look around. Curious faces peered back. Old, young, different colors and heights and—

Cole's head went back. He rubbed his stinging eyes and then focused hard. A little boy in a red tee was walking toward him, a football slotted under his arm, looking for all the world as if nothing had happened, nothing was wrong.

A rush of adrenaline propelled him forward at the same time a cry broke from his lips. Then he was on his knees, hugging his brother so tight that, if it had been anyone else, Cole would have told them to back the hell off.

"Cole? You okay?"

Both cheeks damp, Cole forced himself to draw back. He inhaled through his nose, smelled that peanut-butter smell that was Tate and almost lost the battle not to hug him extra tight again. Was the nightmare truly over?

His throat and voice were thick as molasses. "I lost you for a minute, kiddo."

"I went to see the paddleboats." Tate turned and pointed to the lake and the oblivious couples peddling around. "Wanna try it with me? Looks really fun."

Chest aching, Cole laughed. He thought he might never stop. "It *is* fun. But give me a minute to catch my breath. I was worried."

"Coz you were alone?"

Suddenly exhausted, Cole grinned. "Uh-huh."

His small smile comforting, Tate brought his big brother close again. Patting his back, he said, "Don't worry, Cole. I'll never leave you. I love you. You know that."

"I do. I know." Cole's throat closed more. "But I'm just not around enough to hear it, am I?"

"You can come around more. Lots more. Daddy's not spending so much time at Hunners now. You shouldn't, too."

"You'd look after me?"

Giving a big sigh, Tate held his brother's hand. "And you can make all the noise you want."

That's when Cole's dam cracked wide-open and, in front of a crowd, on his knees in his little brother's arms, the CEO of Hunter Broadcasting surrendered and broke down.

Nineteen

"Thanks for coming with me, sweetie. I know you're busy polishing up your résumé."

Parking her car, Taryn glanced across at her aunt, who was sitting with her best handbag on her lap in the passenger seat.

"Spending the morning with you is tons more fun than sorting out job history and qualifications." *Everything that reminds me how I quit a job I thought I'd love. That I will never again see the man I stupidly fell in love with.*

Taryn switched off the ignition, opened her door and got her thoughts on track. "I'm just wondering when you got interested in nautical themes."

"It's time for a change. I'm over polished oak and tapestry upholstery. When I saw that flyer earlier this week, the stock and colors leaped out and grabbed me."

Taryn checked out the run of storefronts, which paralleled a busy marina. Shielding her eyes from the sun, she inhaled the scent drifting in on a gentle saltwater breeze. Sydney was interlaced with so many gorgeous bays, but this morning, all that clear blue water stretching out toward the "great beyond" made her heart squeeze tight in her chest.

Each day she told herself to focus on tomorrow not on yes-

terday. Having left Hunter Broadcasting for good, the world
was her oyster. She could pursue her dream of producing; she
still believed *Hot Spots* would appeal to a wide audience. On
the other hand, just because she'd worked in TV all her adult
life didn't mean she wouldn't enjoy a different vocation. A job
that would suit her a hundred times more, maybe.

In a place that didn't remind her of Cole.

As they crossed the parking lot, Vi examined that flyer
again.

"According to this, the store's way down the other end. I
only want a quick look, first up. No deposits until I've chewed
over all the options."

They were passing a café, its display cabinet filled with
rows of scrumptious-looking cakes. Taryn wasn't surprised
when Vi's step slowed and she asked, "Want to stop for a coffee before tackling the shops?"

"Sure. I missed my caffeine hit this morning."

"And that torte is calling me. I'll go on ahead for a preliminary once-over of that floor stock, you order us something
nice and I'll meet you back here in ten."

"Take your time."

Taryn headed for an outside table while Vi, in her denim
pedal pushers, hurried away.

After consulting the menu, Taryn passed on her orders to
a waitress: latte and torte for Vi, fresh seasonal berries with
a Muscat cream and a flat white for her. As she sat back and
drank in a view crammed with boats, of course she thought
of Cole again, and of how close she'd come to crumpling and
inviting him back into her life.

Even now when she thought of the way he'd held her that
rainy day at her door—the determination of that sizzling
kiss—she suffered the same doubts. What if Vi were right in
her advice? If she hadn't pushed Cole away that final time,
perhaps that path might have somehow opened for them again.

At some stage Cole must realize he couldn't battle everyone's storms all of the time. Couldn't he cut himself some slack?

Didn't he want his own life?

But as Roman had said, a leopard doesn't change its spots. Cole blustered around, letting all and sundry know how indispensible he was. The kicker was, as far as she was concerned, he *was* special. Incredibly so.

No one else would ever make her pulse race the way he did. When they made love, every move was perfect. Every stroke sublime. This constant gnawing she felt must fade with time but, sitting here now, remembering their amazing night on that quiet moonlit beach, she simply couldn't see it.

Guess there was the possibility she would never fall in love again. Hadn't that been true for Vi? Some people's hearts could only be given away once. With only passersby and squawking gulls for company, Taryn couldn't help imagining going through life alone…with no partner, no children.

No family of her own.

Taryn gazed blindly at her sandals and forced herself to be positive. Common sense said she'd feel so much better in three months. Probably her old self again in six. If only she could stop thinking about how wonderful his mouth had felt grazing over hers. How alive she'd been when they'd laughed together and had opened up. It had felt so…*real*.

A flower blew under the next table—a large red bloom that looked much like the one she admired on that island. Angling, Taryn focused on the petals, the soft scarlet plains. Was everything today meant to remind her of Cole?

About to lean over and collect that flower, Taryn tipped back as cake and berries arrived. But when the plates slid onto the tabletop, she noticed the hands that served her were male. Not uncommon. Except she recognized those hands, the bronzed corded forearms. Oh, God, she knew that watch.

From head to toe she began to tingle. But it couldn't be.

This had to be her imagination running wild. Too much mulling had short-circuited her brain. But then that voice resonated out, drifting like a warm welcome veil over her senses and denial was simply no use.

He asked, "Is there anything else I can do for you?"

As time seemed to slow, Taryn clamped shut her eyes. In a heartbeat, the island and those bittersweet memories were back. A stinging pain penetrated her ribs. How would she ever move on if he kept showing up like this?

When she opened her eyes, that flower was sitting on the table in front of her as if placed there by magic. The impulse to either sweep the bloom aside or hug it close was overwhelming. Her fingers itched to stroke the velvet petals, place them against her cheek and wish them all back to that time.

Instead, she pushed her back into the chair and bit down as a man rounded the table. When their eyes met, Taryn's stomach looped and her head began to prickle with heat, just like the tips of her breasts. In casual white trousers, rubber-soled shoes and a black short-sleeved shirt, Cole gazed down at her as his dark hair rippled in a stiffening breeze.

"Nice view," he said.

She crossed her arms. Found her voice. "I'm waiting for my aunt. She'll be back any moment."

He nodded as if it were of little consequence. "You're looking well."

Taryn didn't feel well, but she noticed that his eyes were clearer than the last time they'd spoken...the last time they'd kissed. And the smudges underneath had faded, too. The strong angle of his jaw was clean-shaven and his expression reflected a completely relaxed air she hadn't seen since their time in the Pacific. Just how had he come to be here this morning, serving her cake when surely he had business to sort?

As if reading her mind, he explained, "I bought a boat."

She'd bite. "Plan to do some cruising around the harbor?"

"Actually, I was planning to set sail for far deeper waters."

"Such as?"

"Ulani."

Taryn blinked. Her *Hot Spots* destination?

"Why there?"

"I have a yearning to see if those turtles hatched and broke out on their own. Must be hell sharing that kind of space with so many siblings."

She looked at him sideways. *Really?* "What happened to all your responsibilities? Has your dad's assailant been caught?"

"Not yet, but I have every faith in Brandon."

"You're not worried something might happen while you're gone?"

"I'll worry. But no more than my brothers and sister. Teagan says she wants to come out."

Taryn started. "You talked to your *sister?*"

He grinned. "It was really good to catch up."

"And what's happening with Tate?"

"He's safe and well. All set to fly over to stay with Dex. I'll stay and keep him company until he does. He hasn't stopped talking about Disneyland."

"But what about your work commitments? The way you spoke, your L.A. section's a hairbreadth away from closing its doors?"

"Yes, well," Cole tugged his ear, "I may have overreacted. I was wrong not to give Dex more credit. Wynn, too. Truth is they're doing their best in hard times."

Taryn couldn't believe she was hearing it. "What brought you to that conclusion?"

"A great big dose of 'appreciate what you have because it could be gone tomorrow.'" He searched her eyes. "Taryn, I need to apologize. You were right. I'd already made my mind up about your show and nothing could change it. But I should have taken a chance. I should have taken a chance on, and believed in, a lot of things."

When his gaze intensified, Taryn's stomach muscles kicked. Pressing a palm against the spot, she switched the focus back onto Cole and this left-field decision to sail off into the sunset.

"And your football contract?" she asked. That was supposed to be critical.

"I finally told Finlay he could jam it," he said. "We signed the next day. We're set there for the next five years."

Taryn was slowly shaking her head. Cole was walking away, just like that? It couldn't be true.

"But you have the everyday running of the place. So many things to oversee—"

"Roman's been given a permanent promotion. He has enough experience in the role. I'm sure he'll do a great job as Hunter Broadcasting's CEO."

Now Taryn was holding her brow. She was happy for Roman but she felt positively dizzy at the news. "I can't believe that you're...that you'll—"

"Leave on a long overdue vacation." Looking so tall and commanding, he cocked his head toward the berths. "Come and take a look at my baby."

For a moment, Taryn felt lost for words. Someone was playing a joke. "You've been brainwashed. Or you fell and hit your head."

"I haven't thought this clearly in years. Come have a look. You don't have to go inside. Just admire her from the jetty."

Her gaze dropping to that flower, Taryn felt her thoughts begin to spin. Cole seemed like a different person. But that wasn't quite right. The man who was smiling and looking so laid-back before her now was the same man she'd fallen for on that island. The person she'd been so drawn to. Was drawn to still.

She schooled her face and her feelings. "Thanks for the invitation, but I'll stay where I am."

Where it's safe.

She collected her spoon and tasted her berries, but Cole didn't take the hint. He didn't leave.

On her second mouthful, he said, "Taryn, I won't blame you if you don't come, but I'm asking you…please. Two minutes, that's all."

Taryn set down her spoon. She knew she ought to stick with no. He couldn't make her go.

Still, what harm could come from taking a quick look?

Besides she was curious.

But when he offered his hand as she moved to stand, she merely got to her feet and walked with him down a pier until they reached a berth that housed an impressive powered catamaran. Her lines were all glossy white, the trimmings gleaming chrome. She was long and the towered flybridge seemed to touch the clouds. Taryn could imagine Cole standing up there, facing the wind and the sea, enjoying the sunshine and battling ocean storms. The name on the boat's side was written in bold blue letters—*BREAK OUT*.

"I thought it was appropriate," he said. Setting his fists low on his hips, he studied his boat from bow to stern. "So, what do you think?"

"She's beautiful."

"*You're* beautiful."

Taryn met his gaze. He was smiling softly, seductively, with that I'm-going-to-kiss-you-soon look sparkling in his eyes.

So not happening.

"I'm sure you'll enjoy many pleasant voyages together," she said, edging away, feeling a smoldering quiver build in her stomach. "I really should get back."

"Want to come along?"

Her mouth dropped open. Cole meant on his trip? He *had* gone mad.

"No," she told him. "I do not want to come along."

"I had the carpenters build a mini quarters for the cats inside."

She blinked several times, let out a short sharp laugh. "Cole, firstly I don't think you could take cats on a boat. They'd jump off and drown." Surely.

"Then I'll take them."

At the sound of that third voice, Taryn pivoted around.

Vi stood close enough to have heard the conversation. Her aunt shrugged. "You know how I love cats."

Taryn could only stare. Was this some kind of conspiracy?

When she got her breath back, Taryn asked her aunt, "You knew about this, didn't you? You purposely led me down here so that Cole could run into me."

Cole intervened. "I contacted Vi and asked for her help."

Taryn couldn't remember an occasion when Vi had lied to her before. Honesty had always been the best policy in their house. But on a deeper level, looking into Vi's apologetic yet hopeful face now, she believed her aunt was sincerely doing what she thought best. She didn't want her niece to throw away what might prove to be her only chance of real happiness. But Taryn had already made up her own mind about that, and she intended to stick with it.

She headed off. "I'm done."

But before she reached Vi, she ran into a man—a delivery guy by his uniform.

The man asked, "Are you Taryn Quinn?"

She frowned then nodded. "Who wants to know?"

He simply handed over his delivery—an enormous, fragrant bouquet. And not just any bunch of flowers. They were big bright scarlet blooms, like the one that boy had given her on the island, like the one she'd found under that café table moments ago.

A jet of emotion filled her chest, her throat. Then her eyes were stinging with the threat of real tears. This was not fair. Was Cole this desperate to get her back into his bed? To snag a sleeping buddy on his Pacific voyage? She wasn't that easily bought, no matter what he might think.

She was ready to swing around and hand these flowers back to the person who had obviously arranged for them to arrive, when another deliveryman strode up, and another. Both were holding similar bouquets. And the men and flowers kept coming. When she couldn't possibly hold any more, Cole directed the men to arrange them on the deck of his boat.

Gobsmacked, Taryn inspected the end of the pier. There must have been ten florist vans lined up. Deliverymen were still traveling down the pier, conveying her very own private world full of petals.

While she choked back emotion, Cole took the bouquets from her arms and handed them over to be laid out with the rest. Then he found her hands and, lifting one at a time, tenderly kissed the back of each wrist.

"Other than my mother, I've never so much as given a daisy to a woman before."

A hot tear slipped from the corner of her eye. She remembered. "You give jewelry."

"I want to give you a piece now."

She stepped back. "But I don't want anything from you."

He closed the space separating them. "This isn't a trick, Taryn. There's no need to be afraid." He smiled. "I'm not."

From a back trouser pocket, he withdrew a small velvet-covered box. He opened the lid then angled the box around for her to see what lay inside.

A large diamond sat at the heart of the ring's setting. Two

Ceylon sapphires, the color of their island's bay, hugged the main stone on either side.

"You're that one special person I've been waiting for," Cole told her. "The woman I want to have as my wife. To bear my children." He grinned. "When we're not sailing the high seas, that is."

"B-but your work," she stammered. "Your family commitments." She knew what he'd told her, but she couldn't believe it.

"From this day forward, I intend to take on board and cherish life's biggest responsibility. To love and care for the woman I adore." One hand took hers. "Taryn, I can't sleep, can't eat, can barely think when you're not around. I need you in my life. As my partner. As my friend."

He slipped the ring on her finger then set that palm against the sandpaper rough of his jaw as his eyes searched hers and he waited for her response.

Taryn was drawn by the steam of his body, the determination of his will. Then she glanced back. Vi's gaze was upon her, her hands and bag clasped at her breasts while she obviously wished only the best for the grown woman who would always be her child. Behind her aunt, all those deliverymen were waiting, leaning on rails or against their vans. And a curious crowd had gathered, too, shoppers she'd watched pass by, the waitress who had taken her order. All were hanging out for her reply. Yes. Or no. Taryn swallowed deeply then slowly turned back.

She thought of her torment these past days then she thought of how bright and clear the future suddenly looked. As Cole's brow pinched a little and more of his heart shone in his eyes, she took a breath and confessed....

"I'm in love with you." Her sigh came out half sob, half laugh of sheer joy. "I can't believe this is happening."

He didn't waste a second. In a heartbeat, she was wrapped

up in his arms and he was telling her, "This is only the start. Our beginning." He pulled away enough to see her face, the tears of joy running down her cheeks. "I was thinking maybe a ceremony at sea. But it's your call." He grinned. "You're in charge."

"With a honeymoon on *Break Out?*" Salty trails curled under her chin. Given all those flowers, she warned him, "I don't think there's any room on that boat left for us."

"I gave the florist explicit instructions to leave the bunk free."

"That's where we sleep?"

His mouth brushed and tickled her ear. "Besides other things."

Cole swept her up into his arms. With the marina filled with vocal cheering well-wishers, he carried her aboard. Standing on the deck with her still in the cradle of his arms, he told her, "There's a tradition for future newlyweds."

Running an adoring hand over the square of his jaw, she murmured, "Give me a hint."

"I'll give you more than that."

With a wicked smile, he lifted her higher and then his mouth claimed hers. She was aware of hoots and cheers going up from the pier. But she was more aware of the promise of the future in her fiancé's kiss. Their life together would never be dull. Could never come second. All their tomorrows would only ever feel warm and safe and loved.

Epilogue

Later in Los Angeles...

Dex Hunter pushed aside his cheeseburger and fries to check out an alert on his phone. When he opened the text, he nearly choked on his food. Receiving a message to say expect a wedding invitation wasn't anything out of the ordinary, and he could've understood if this was news from his *younger* brother. Wynn had been seeing someone steadily for a couple of years now.

But if a woman had convinced *Cole,* the eldest, to walk down the aisle, she must be a special lady, indeed. Dex looked forward to meeting—

He flicked to the top of the message for a name.

Taryn Quinn.

And it looked as if the *youngest* of the Hunter clan—five-year-old Tate—was about to pay that visit, which meant finally making good on that promise to do Disneyland. Tate was expected in L.A. a week from today.

Dex's face fell and he spluttered on a mouthful of coffee. One week!

He brought up his calendar, starting this Sunday. A premiere he couldn't miss, a couple of charity events, meetings with financial directors... *Oh, joy.* He'd just need to rearrange some things, was all. *And* hire a babysitter for Tate, Dex thought as he lifted his cup again. Didn't matter what she looked like, as long as she was maternal and tuned in to his little brother's whirlwind personality. Hell, she could be old and toothless for all he cared. Hairy and bowlegged, made no difference to him.

A thump on his back sent Dex's espresso splashing over the tablecloth. The dropped cup clattered into its saucer as Dex shook out his scorched wet hand and a concerned voice came from behind.

"Oh, no. Oh, God, are you all right?"

A waitress with luxurious hair, the color of polished mahogany and set in pigtails, skirted around to stand before him. Wearing white flats and a uniform that offered little justice to her obvious curves, she dragged a cloth from her apron's pouch and dabbed at his hand and his sleeve.

"Please don't tell anyone," she whispered, darting a nervous glance around. Her eyes were green, bright and fringed with naturally thick lashes. "I've already dropped a plate of tacos today."

Dex didn't fall back on his obvious and, in his case, warranted, line too often. However, now he couldn't help but ask.

"Have you ever considered a career in movies?"

She kept dabbing. "I couldn't act my way out of a paper bag. I didn't come to L.A. for that. Although I have put my name down at a couple of agencies."

Dex cocked a brow. So she was new to town? When she straightened, he took in her height, those cheekbones—that aura—and surmised. "Modeling."

"*Nannying.* I want to work with kids." She flashed a big white smile. "Children like me. I like them, too."

Smiling back, already making plans, Dex pulled out a business card. Someone was watching over him today. Clearly this union was meant to be.

* * * * *

Watch for Dex's story, the next in
THE HUNTER PACT series,
coming from Harlequin Desire in 2013!